UNDER THE INFLUENCE

A NOVEL

BY

HILARY ROSE BODIFORD

Under the Influence

Published by The Yellow Bird Press, 139 W Luke Ave. Summerville, SC 29483

ISBN (paperback) 978-1-7339449-5-3
ISBN (EBOOK) 978-1-7339449-6-0

Cover Art: Nicole Seitz
Author Photo: Nicole Mickle

For the first six people who read this story.

"It's a very difficult era in which to be a person, just a real, actual person, instead of a collection of personality traits selected from an endless Automat of characters."

—Gillian Flynn, *Gone Girl*

PROLOGUE

VIRGINIA

Someone with an untrained eye might mistake me for one of them. My appearance, my clothes, my car, my watch, they're all there. Close enough, anyway. It's me that's off, myself, as a person. You really have to know your stuff to tell the difference between them and me, but the problem is, most people around here do. Since the day they were brought home from the hospital in their $700 car seat strapped into their parents' $100,000 new Range Rover, they've been dunked in the pool of unlimited resources and opportunities. If their appearance wasn't right, they could change it (and they did). Nose jobs, highlights, IPL facials, personal trainers, the works. The question of having the right stuff wasn't even a question, really. They can have whatever they want. Everything about this world comes naturally to them, and they grew up elbow to elbow with their blonde clones in the halls of their private schools.

As for me, I somehow stumbled into this world, and ever since, I've had to work my ass off just to keep up. But if they don't get to know me too well, if I keep them at arm's length, I'm certain I'll be able to pull this off. I don't want to be a normal person; I want to be like them. All that matters is the perception. The chances of us meeting is slim—it's my life online they'll get to know.

All I have to do is convince myself that I belong here too. Start from the inside and the illusion will work its way out. I just have to treat myself as if I have been here all along, and I know that I will convince them as well. To me, there is no other option. My sights are set.

I will be one of them. No, not just one of them, I'm going to be the best.

CHAPTER 1

February 26, 2020

Charleston, SC

VIRGINIA

As I lean against the soft fabric of our kitchen chairs, I look off into the living room. I can smell the scent of the burnt wood from a fire Bennett made last night as classical piano softly dances around the room. I feel his dark eyes on me, but I ignore his gaze and continue to scan the room for comforting objects. The comfy couch where we sit together and watch *The Office* on his nights off. The photo on the wall of Bennett on one knee proposing to me beneath the warm orange sunset sky last fall. The weighted blanket I bought myself last month strewn carefully over our blue upholstered accent chair. Our tall fiddle leaf fig tree standing proudly next to the picture window, displaying only a few browned leaves. The shelves that he made with his own hands on the back wall holding my mountains of books.

I turn toward him, sitting uncomfortably across from me at the table. His face wrinkles with concern as he studies me, knowing I'm having one of my moments.

My phone is clutched tightly in both hands on my lap, shining its light with familiar faces on my feed staring up at me.

I can feel the band of my engagement ring digging into my finger, but I hardly notice the dull pain. To be honest, my hangover headache hurts worse.

Much worse.

I meet Bennett's eyes and flip my internal switch. I won't be that girl tonight. He's just spent an hour creating the delicious meal in front of me, fried chicken and green bean casserole. Cooking was never my strong suit and not really worth my time to learn. I decide I won't spoil the night by having a meltdown. I squint my eyes into a forced but convincing smile.

"This looks amazing! How does it feel to be a man of so many talents?" I'm impressed by how genuinely happy I sound with this witty remark. My fork clinks against the white dinner plate as I scoop up another bite.

Straightening up in his chair, Bennett joins in my smile as he grabs for his fork and knife to dig in. "It's a tough job, but someone's gotta do it." He laughs as he chews on the generous bite of casserole. His wide shoulders work against his South Carolina Gamecocks dry fit shirt as he cuts into his serving of chicken.

I make an enthusiastic *mmmm* noise as I chew to further convince him that I'm fine, then sneak a quick look down at my phone again. The red notification in the right-hand corner of the home page taunts me unrelentingly. 104 unread messages. I can't delete them fast enough, and even as I do, the unforgiving first line is visible and I can't help but read it every time.

You are DISGUSTING! It makes m...

How dare you? She doesn't dese...

Why don't you just die you whor...

My eyes squeeze shut as I hold back the frustrated tears that are sure to pour out as soon as I'm alone, but I don't close my phone.

What do they call it when you can't get enough of the pain? Sadist or masochist? I don't bother trying to figure it out right now. My arm habitually reaches for my tall glass of pinot noir, and I gulp down a big sip and let the numbing elixir do its work. Under my false lashes I blink up to catch Bennett's eyes across the table again. I can feel his sympathy reaching across our blue and white china to embrace me, but it doesn't help. He couldn't possibly understand what this is like. I've dedicated too much of my life to being an influencer, and I was so close to making it past a certain threshold of success before this nightmare happened.

I quickly look back down for one final scroll on my feed and promise myself I'll put my phone down for the night after this. To my dismay, the last people I want to see now fill my screen.

Their faces paralyze me. They always have. No matter what news they bring to my Instagram feed, a knot will fill my stomach. Good news? They'll receive a mountain of praise. Bad news? They'll get an equally vast amount of sympathy and support by the hundreds of new faces they recruit to their brand per day. I've seen these two faces looking back at me from my phone for years now, but tonight it's different. It's been different for a while.

I will myself to read the caption beneath the two smiling blondes, and suddenly, I'm numb. A ringing rises in my ears. I catch my breath as a knot fills my chest. It drops to my stomach with an ache so heavy that for a second I forget how to exhale.

My mouth opens to speak but nothing comes out. In a jerking motion my phone is now inches from my face as my shaking hands work to hold it as steady as possible so my eyes can understand the words I'm reading.

"Babe, what is it?" Bennett must have noticed my sudden change, and I hear the clang of his silverware hit the plate as he rises from his seat and moves toward me.

"Virginia? Come on, show me!"

Staring straight ahead, I place the phone in his hands for him to see, but Nella Rose's words continue to echo in my mind on a loop.

My heart is broken. My incredible friend, Iris Sutten, the girl who taught me everything. The girl who was like a sister to me. The girl who has always been there for me, is no longer with us...

Iris, dead?

No way.

She's really *dead*?

CHAPTER 2

March 8, 2020

Mount Pleasant, SC

NELLA ROSE

I seriously can't even believe this shit is happening to me. Five squad cars and a slew of TV vans sit outside the house, and all I can think about is how glad I am that I did that three-day juice cleanse, which Patrick convinced me to do. When I'm stressed, all I can think about is Taco Bell, but he's always had a special talent for bringing me down to earth.

"You'll be happy you looked your best," he had said as he unpacked the bottles of various colored juices a few days back, designed for a quick fat flush. My back turned to him, I poured down the drain the remaining scotch in my iced tea glass before he could ask what was in it.

I look over at my husband who's peering through the shades at the spectacle happening on our long circle drive. I don't think this many cops have ever been in Plantation Meadows at the same time in its entire creation. One of the reasons we moved here and pay the $1,000 HOA fees every year is that it's the nicest neighborhood in Mount Pleasant and the safest place we could bring up our girls. Not like other nice neighborhoods someone might imagine though. Here, the word "nice" is hardly sufficient.

This neighborhood is established with huge oak trees throughout. Even the smaller lots could easily fit at least two mature oak trees in their yard. We have seven total, and I have been trying to convince Patrick to buy the small 2-acre lot next to ours so we could have a decent-sized guest house. If that works out, we'd have ten oaks. Each house in the neighborhood is different, distinct, not like those puzzle piece new neighborhoods where every home is a carbon copy of the next with the exception of a paint color. I'm sure that's nice for some people, but it's just not us. No, here every home has its own extravagant charm—classic Charleston singles, circa 1800 Victorians, 1950's brick ranches and original plantation style homes, like ours—each on their own plot of land never smaller than a quarter of an acre. While some are new builds with modern exteriors (built by screenwriters and casting agents moving to get away from the bustle of L.A.), the best are the ones like mine, the homes that have been here since the neighborhood's creation in the 1700s but have been renovated into classic but modern mansions. Only necessary renovations, of course, carefully moderated by the city council to ensure the exteriors remain authentic.

I turn back to the front yard where we had the landscapers come by yesterday to spruce everything up, but they totally forgot to tend to the rose bushes. They look like shit. I make a mental note to call them tomorrow.

Compared to the chatter of voices outside, it's quiet in our big house. Eleanor and Corinne are with their grandma for the day, Patrick insisted. Not that they would be making too much noise since the nanny always keeps them pretty occupied on the weekends with trips to the Charleston Aquarium or Sullivan's Island beach.

"Is this actually happening?" I breathe as I turn to Patrick standing at the window next to me, clutching a white linen curtain panel.

"It'll be over before you know it. Of course, they're going to question you; y'all are…er…were best friends. You spent practically every day together." I can feel the weight of his hand on my shoulder for a brief instant before he retrieves it and stuffs it in the pocket of his khaki slacks. My stiletto heels cause a creak in our hardwood floors as I take a step away from him. That's the cue for the lawyer.

"Don't worry, Nella." Our lawyer's stilettos tap across the marble floor of the dining room as she approaches us. "As long as we show them your picture-perfect life as a mother and wife and your friendship with Iris and stay away from the topic of your social media, you'll be fine." Taylor Wright is ready for business in her smart separates, slightly bulging over her middle-aged natural stomach flab.

I'm annoyed she left out the "Rose" in my name—it's Nella Rose, a double name, but so many people forget it I let it slide. No use, she won't be directing the questioning in this interview.

"I just don't understand why this has to be televised," says Patrick. "I've never heard of anything like that. They say she's not a suspect, yet they're doing an interview about Iris to… what? Just get more information about their relationship? We should have never agreed to this." Patrick is starting to lose his cool. "Why the need to draw this kind of attention?"

Taylor takes a step toward us with her hands raised slightly in a *calm down* motion.

"She was a presence here in Charleston and the surrounding areas," she says. "It's totally normal that they want to do a segment on her on the local news channel. Lots of people are wondering what happened to her. I'm just here to be sure they keep the questioning friendly so you don't accidentally say anything that could lead them to add you to their suspect list. Remember, you're not at the police station. You're not a person of interest, and this is not an interrogation."

"Then why isn't a journalist doing the damn interview instead of the lead detective?!" Patrick is turning the same shade of the cherry tomatoes in the caprese salad our chef made.

"All they told me is that it added an interesting element to the segment. I don't think it's anything to worry about." Taylor has taken a step back, Patrick's temper tantrum must be a strange sight to someone who doesn't know him like I do.

The doorbell rings and my heart completely stops. I wasn't as nervous before, but Patrick's energy has seeped into me.

Taylor tucks a piece of straight, dirty blonde hair behind her ear, her roots in desperate need of a touchup. She nods and pivots to approach the front door. She stops and looks back our way before she opens it.

"Okay, whenever y'all are ready," she says. Only in South Carolina would an educated woman like

Taylor Wright use the word “y’all” in everyday conversation.

I walk over to the large, floor-length gilded mirror in the foyer, a wedding present from Patrick’s grandmother. I smooth out my hair and the nonexistent creases in my lavender Rebecca Taylor midi dress. It has a high neckline with a delicate lace collar accentuated by my long neck. My reflection stares back at me with worried eyes, but there’s no time to calm down. They’re here.

“I’m ready.”

CHAPTER 3

September 3, 2019

Charleston, SC

VIRGINIA

With three huge suitcases full of more envy-worthy outfits than I should need (but I will), I'm ready for my trip. I couldn't resist this invite. My first of the kind.

I'm going to New York Fashion Week with them.

The Virginia they get to hang out with this weekend (@Meetvirginialane) is "*SO SWEET*" and "*ADORABLE*" and "*THE CUTEST HUMAN*" and she fits right in with all the other perky twenty-somethings with an above-average presence on social media. Or, at least they'll pretend to my face. They'll *love* her and end the weekend with kisses on the cheek and plans for a fabulous beach vacation in February to get ahead of the bikini sales. That's the Virginia they get to meet, and she's pretty great. Get to know her too well, though, and you might not be so eager to confirm that booking for three nights in Aruba. She's probably not what you thought she was based on what you see online.

"You sure you packed enough fur coats? I'm sure you have another suitcase around here you can fill up."

Oh, Bennett. Coming in hot with the jokes and it's only 7 a.m.

"They're *faux* fur, B. I'm not a monster," I say to the mirror as I lather more thick full-coverage foundation to cover my lovely zits that decided to pop up this week. How I miss the days when makeup like this was saved only for special occasions. For the last three years, it's been a five-day per week situation.

"Can you take that smart-ass of yours and put it to use? I need to get these bags downstairs." I try to keep the energy light.

He lets out a small chuckle. He's always liked when I mess with him like that.

Studying myself in the mirror, I finish blending the makeup. I think I look pretty decent. My brown eyes are so dark they almost look black. I've got a proportionate nose, high cheekbones (a little hidden in the eight to ten pounds I want to lose), naturally tanned skin thanks to my mom, and decent lips and good skin, thanks to $50 face-wash and an abundance of oils and moisturizers I lather on every night religiously. My hair is long (no extensions needed, it's always been pretty long) with some lightly painted caramel balayage. *Good enough* is what comes to mind when I see myself, but I suspect I'll never be fully happy with my appearance when photographed next to them in New York.

These girls definitely don't eat tacos, and if they do, they'll work them off the next day at a $350/month Barre membership.

Bennett always said he loved the way I looked, but I don't know. I'm pretty hard on myself. I am very into his looks, though. His 6'5" frame towers over me, and his freckled broad shoulders are my biggest weakness. I smile to myself as I think about him, and I peek out the bathroom door to see what he's doing in there. He's not the kind to get caught up in all this. He's a simple man who I know is attracted to me but also loves me for me.

He'd be fine if I never wore makeup again.

Grabbing the handle on one of the massive cases, I catch a glimpse as he rolls it toward the door. He lifts his head when he notices me in the doorway, but he turns and asks with his back to me, fumbling with the handle, "So, who's going to be there?"

Continuing to blend the foundation, I don't miss a beat. He knows what he's doing by acting casually about it.

"Um, you know Iris and Nella Rose, right?" As if there was a world where he wouldn't know exactly who I'm talking about.

Through the corner of my eye I can see his pensive face thinking through his next move. He's confused. For all he knows, Iris and I haven't spoken (in person) in a really long time, maybe a year, and now I'm suddenly going on a trip with her. And not just her, Nella Rose, too. All he knows about her is what I've told him, which is just that she and Iris are best friends and that I thought she didn't like me at all.

He doesn't know about Iris' random text to me about a month ago, being really nice, and how that conversation led to her asking me to come to New York. I was shocked, but at the risk of closing the door on this possible friendship, I agreed. I finally got an invite to go on a trip with them. I made it on their exclusive list, one as air-tight as the member list at the Soho House, after living in the same city as them for over three years and never getting asked to go on as much as a coffee date. Everyone in my world knows that hitching your wagon to someone like Iris is your ticket to success, no matter how mediocre you are. I see it happen all the time. Real friendships existed between nice, authentic girls, but more often than not, you could tell that many of them were just using each other. It's usually the ones who were exclusively friends with other bloggers, instead of keeping up any old friendships they had before their career started. It's rare to see real growth and success in anyone who doesn't go this route.

You would have had to watch closely to see how Nella Rose did it with Iris. It happened too long ago, but it happened. Nella Rose was a nobody, then she became friends with Iris and suddenly she skyrocketed because they did everything together and Iris tagged her in everything, and other than her ridiculous wealth she really didn't have much going for her. Not enough to become where she is now, anyway.

I glance at my makeup bag to be sure I packed the necessary medication that will present me at my very best during such an occasion. I have as good of a chance as Nella Rose, and, I mean, who am I to turn down a possible key?

"That'll be fun. I'm sure it's nice to have someone there that you know. I feel like you're always meeting up with strangers."

He knows what must be going on in my head right now, but I know he's trying to play it cool for me so I won't be more nervous than I already am.

"Yeah, it'll be fun." Did that sound chill? I can't tell.

His footsteps are heavy down the stairs as he lugs my heavy bags. I quickly finish up my face and zip the remainder of my products in my makeup bag as a heavy sigh leaves my body.

Can I really pull this off?

The Uber pulls up and Bennett carefully loads my bags in the trunk like a game of Tetris as I follow him out to the curb. It's a little cooler out for September in the south, and I don't look as ridiculous as usual in my sweater and jeans. A normal person would be wearing shorts in 78-degree weather, but not a blogger. People are only buying fall clothes right now, so that's what I have to wear. We are always one season ahead. Bennett opens the back door of the Uber for me and pauses, blocking my entry. Staring just below my face, probably at the floating diamond necklace he got me for Valentine's Day this year, I feel his hand reach out and touch my shoulder gently.

"Have fun and let me know if you need anything, babe."

My best fake smile stretches across my face as I reach up to him for a hug.

"I will. I love you!"

CHAPTER 4

March 8, 2020

Mount Pleasant, SC

NELLA ROSE

"So, why don't we start from the beginning, Nella."

Again, *really*?

"It's Nella Rose, actually." I smile.

Oh, no. That sounded too abrasive. But this is going on TV after all. I want it to be right.

The detective, who I've learned is Detective Madeline Holliday, flashes insanely white teeth through a cherry-red lipstick smile. Matte finish. Her red hair brings out her yellow-green eyes, and as she tucks a thick lock of it behind her ear with a perfectly manicured hand, I'm suddenly aware of how dull my brown eyes are, but I'm glad I had my extensions freshened up a few weeks ago. I finger my long platinum blonde strands and try to remain confident. Deep breaths and smiles.

"I'm so sorry, Nella *Rose*. Pretty name. Let's start from the beginning. Can you tell me how long you knew Iris?"

The TV camera blinks a red light at me as I steal a look toward Patrick in the corner of the room to avoid the crowds of people standing around, sipping coffee and eating the snacks I set out for everyone. I don't get why so many people showed up when it's just going to be for one news channel. Patrick's pulled out one of our oak dining room chairs and sits with his elbows on his knees and his hands brought together in a fist. He gives me an encouraging nod.

"Yes, it's been about five years. We met through blogging at an event for the opening of a new restaurant." I attempt my sweetest smile in her direction. All I have to do is tell the truth, I keep reminding myself. She won't ask the tough questions. She doesn't know anything about our friendship.

"And how would you describe your relationship with Iris upon the time of her death?" The detective states the word death in such a neutral manner, like an axe murderer, really. Shouldn't there be more cutesie questions to get us started? I stay even.

"Iris and I have always been extremely close. I've considered her my best friend since the beginning, and we have only grown closer since we both moved to Mount Pleasant. We actually got married within a year of each other, and our kids are the same age." I suddenly feel like that statement should have been more emotional. I try to recall something sad to make my eyes water and it works. I gently raise a hand to my left eye and carefully dab a small tear that's trickled down, careful not to mess up my makeup."That's so sweet," grins Detective Holliday. I can't tell if that was sincere. She continues,"Can you tell me, more specifically, if you can recall the nature of your relationship in the last *few weeks* before her death?"

"I'm sorry," I say, suddenly panicking at the directness of this question. My heart starts to race and I look around the room to see the faces of the crew. They all stand there like robots.

“Um, I don’t understand. What exactly do you mean by that?” I am trained in the art of false enthusiasm, so my question doesn’t sound too bad.

“Well, new information about the case has recently been discovered. Of course, I can’t relay the exact details to you here at this time, but what I can say is that myself and my team now have reason to believe that the person who took Iris’ life was likely a woman.” Detective Holliday remains calm, delivering her line expertly without the slightest hint of emotion.

I can feel myself unhinging. Is she allowed to drop this kind of information on me like this? I give myself another second to compose. I need to get through this.

I begin carefully. “That’s crazy to think a woman would do that to another woman, especially someone as wonderful as Iris. She and I have always been best friends. The nature of our relationship has never changed, and definitely not in the last few weeks of her life. What would *we* have to argue about?”

The detective smiles again. “Okay then, that’s really nice to hear. Especially being in the same career, I would have guessed some jealousy might have come in between you. But then again I don’t know much about your field.”

What is she saying? What could she possibly know about my *career*? She might be beautiful, but anyone can save up for one pair of Louboutins. I doubt she has been inside a house like ours in her entire life. I don’t know how to answer her remark, so I look over to my lawyer and she looks at the detective.

“Unless you want to stop this now and take my client to the station for questioning as an official person of interest, we need to keep this light, Detective,” Taylor says with agitation.

Detective Holliday looks my way with a smile and doesn’t argue with Taylor. I don’t know enough about a murder case to understand if what Holliday was doing was legal or not, but I’m assuming she was flirting with the line based on Taylor’s reaction. Or maybe she was just bluffing.

"Of course. So, Nella Rose, tell us your favorite thing about Iris."

"Oh my gosh, there are so many things." I rack my brain for something compelling. "I guess, I'd have to say how much I loved her spirit. She was always so passionate and fun; it was intoxicating to be around. It's something I miss deeply."

Holliday makes a note on a pad she's holding in her lap and nods.

"That's very nice. I'm sure a lot of people miss that about her."

CHAPTER 5

September 3, 2019

New York, NY

VIRGINIA

My taxi rounds the corner, and my hotel stands tall and opulent amidst other similarly-styled buildings on this street. The anxiety immediately sets in, its hot and shrill power covering my body like an itchy wool blanket you'd find at a Pigeon Forge mountain house. Digging in my Neverfull bag, I dry swallow a Zoloft before it can completely take me away into the darkness. I close my eyes tight. *Breathe deep.* I should have taken it earlier.

Echoing in my ear, I repeat what I've been telling myself ever since I got the invitation from Iris.

Be like them.

Make them like me.

Have more followers.

Get more likes.

Make more money.

Be better than them.

And if I'm better, I'll be happy. I know it.

I grab for my phone next. Time for another dose of medication, one I can't find in a bottle.

I check my page, hoping for the sweet satisfaction of acceptance from my followers, which can sometimes be much stronger than anything I can get from my pharmacist.

20 new followers.

3,690 likes and 210 comments on my travel outfit photo from this morning.

27 DM's asking who I was going to NYC with.

They're decent enough numbers for me, but it doesn't quite give me the gratification I need. I thought I would hit 200,000 followers before I arrived today but it's no sail. I sit at 198,000.

I lock my phone and hold it in my lap on top of my blush pink sweater dress. Bennett gave me his credit card to prepare for the trip, knowing if I had the right clothes I would feel more at ease. Hence all the suitcases. I had been raised to shop discount all my life. First out of necessity, then out of habit and what my mother would call *just good sense*. Not one of my non-blogger friends would have dropped the kind of money I did on my outfits for this trip, but that's just part of this gig. Well, in this circle anyway. There aren't any of those girls who made their entire brand out of affordable Target and Amazon finds on this trip or in Mount Pleasant, for that matter. I can hang with those girls.

Slouching in my seat, I lay my head back, close my eyes and repeat to myself: *You can do this; they're just people. They're just people. You will fit right in.*

"We're here, Miss."

I jerk a bit as my eyes pop back open. "Oh, yes, thank you. Can you please help me with my bags?" I hate sounding like that, but I don't want to roll up to this hotel clumsily yanking my bags out of the trunk.

The cab driver huffs out what I can only guess is a "fuck you" in Russian and heaves his heavy frame out of the car. The seat creaks. I hand him a five as the bellman takes over from the cab driver and loads my three suitcases onto the luggage cart. Holding onto my purse, I look inside at my pill bottle as I return my wallet to its zipper pocket. I shake another tiny while capsule into my hand and swallow. That should do it. The bellman leads me through the gold-trimmed revolving door.

Shit. They're already at the desk. I can see their wavy blonde heads bouncing from all the way across the lobby. Iris and her sidekick are hard to miss. Frantically grabbing for my phone, my heart rate quickens as I open the camera to check out the damage from the three-hour flight. God bless stay-all-day foundation and my naturally wavy hair. I planned on making a stop in the lobby bathroom to touch myself up before seeing everyone , but looks like the time is now. I look decent enough for a greeting.

"Ginny!!" One of the blonde heads shrieks.

I take in a ragged breath. *Let's do this.*

CHAPTER 6

March 8, 2020

Mount Pleasant, SC

NELLA ROSE

“I don’t think that could have gone any better.” Patrick’s voice echoes across our great room.

I see him swirl his favorite scotch in a crystal glass as he sits in his big leather chair. Nothing without his routines, you can find him in this exact position almost every night. He watches me while I clean away the food we had out for the news crew and lawyers as he takes a small sip. He’s trying to read me, but we both know how that will turn out.

“Don’t you think that detective was coming on a little strong? Everyone tells me I’m not actually a serious suspect.” I frown. No one touched this caprese salad. That was $500 worth of catering for nothing. I scrape the sticky remains in the trash. A bit of balsamic vinaigrette touches my pinky. I lick it. That's all I'll allow.

Normally our housekeeper would be doing chores like this, but I know it annoys Patrick to see me sitting around on my phone while the help does the kitchen work.

"Come on. It doesn't matter how any of this goes. You didn't do it, they have no proof, so there's nothing to be worried about." He takes another sip and overly-exaggerates an exhale.

We are both very used to this routine. We have been doing it for years. I act as if nothing is wrong and he acts like I have nothing to be upset about. He doesn't *deal well with emotional females*. That's what he likes to say. Sounds like a cliché line from a 1950's movie.

I don't feel like carrying on a conversation tonight, but I have to remind him about tomorrow. "Um, don't forget. I have some girls coming over for the remembrance thing for Iris tomorrow."

My back is to him as I continue with the dishes, but I can feel the tension from him all the way in the other room. He hates it when I have guests over, but this little event was important to plan for a lot of reasons.

"Oh, right. Who's coming?" His voice is as calm and level as the ocean water outside our window in the early morning.

I start on the coffee mugs. There's a bright red lipstick stain that refuses to wipe away, no doubt from Taylor, or maybe Detective Holliday.

"Um, Lauren and Virginia for sure." *Virginia*, I couldn't get away with not inviting her. "Maybe Mary. I think Grayson will be in the Hamptons. Sydney and Tarah said they might show up if they can get a sitter. You know, just the girls around town."

"Gotcha." He sounds bored. Why did he even ask?

I hear the leather groan as he gets up from his chair and walks toward me. I keep my back turned and continue with the dishes. Maybe he is coming to apologize. Maybe he will take me in his arms and make me forget everything he put me through over the last few months. A few days after every fight we've had, he's always come to me and convinced me things would get better. He knew he could keep me this way, how just a few kind words were all it took to make me forget.

He knows how just one kind gesture can be the only thing that holds me together.

I hear his footsteps come closer to me across our wood floors. He places his glass on the marble counter with a clink, next to the sink and not in it, and passes behind me toward the stairs on his way to our bedroom without a word.

CHAPTER 7

September 3, 2019

New York, NY

VIRGINIA

"IRIS! NELLA ROSE!"

Iris half jogs toward me in the giant marble lobby of the hotel with her phone camera facing me. She's recording for her stories.

"Look who's heeeeere! It's Virginia!" Iris is gushing with excitement that's so intoxicating it's on the verge of infuriating. Is she really excited to see me? Why now, all of a sudden? Even jogging across a hotel she looks perfect. (I know I wouldn't look like that).

Throwing up my hands in an excited wave I yell, "I'm so excited I'm finally here!" She tosses her phone in her quilted YSL and throws her arms around me for one of those huge girl hugs, the kind where they think the harder they squeeze you the more they care. I hug her back with the same force.

Nella Rose follows swiftly behind Iris, still smiling, but not as big. She's always level, composed. She's not the kind to elbow people out of her way to run in for a huge hug. Her long blonde hair (just a shade different than Iris', a little warmer) cascades over both her slender shoulders in soft, immaculate waves. She's wearing distressed boyfriend jeans with a frayed hem and a tank top under a lavender chunky sweater hanging off one shoulder. Gold David Yurman bracelets, more than should be allowed, hang on her wrist above a shiny diamond tennis bracelet and that huge pink diamond ring. I looked up her ring once. It's estimated to cost about half a million dollars. She bats her eyelashes at me and smiles perfect white teeth through lightly-glossed lips. She looks perfect. I look down at my outfit, hoping maybe she thinks the same about me, though I doubt it.

"I'm so glad we decided to do this. It's been way too long!" she says as she one-arm hugs my waist, holding her own Neverfull in her other hand. I tower over her (I'm 5'8", and she can't be more than 5'3"), but I can still smell the strong and familiar scent of self-tanning lotion. Leave it to a blogger to make sure she's perfectly summer-tanned even in September.

"I know! And what perfect timing." I'm smiling so big, I can feel my eyes squint. I look my most non-threatening and genuine like this.

The bellman follows our trio of chattering birds down the hall with the luggage cart, and Iris thanks him with a ten once we arrive at the room. I plop on the bed by the window, already knowing Iris and Nella Rose will be the ones to share the bed. They live on the same side of the bridge (a Charleston term—every area is defined by what bridge you cross to get where—"The bridge" is the Ravenel Bridge from downtown Charleston to Mount Pleasant). They both moved to Mount Pleasant with their husbands while I stayed downtown with Bennett. We wanted to rent for a few years before buying a house on James Island, my idea of course.

Bennett had always loved Mount Pleasant, but I convinced him that we could get more bang for our buck if we bought a house near the marsh on James Island.

"Virginia, get changed, girlfriend. We've got dinner rezzies!" Iris unzips her suitcase and starts carefully retrieving gorgeous clothing pieces to hang up in the closet, a blush fur coat that looks so soft I want to bury my face in it (Faux? Probably not.), a pair of leather leggings, a camel sweater dress, a plaid pea coat. Way too many outfits than she'll actually need come pouring out, and I panic as I consider the eight outfits I bought for the three-day trip. The sound of heavy wooden hotel hangers being taken from the rod then replaced, sporting elegant item after elegant item, fills the room. I knew I should have packed more, but I felt guilty enough for the hefty charge I put on Bennett's card as it was.

"I hope we can fit everything in this closet! Iris, I told you we should have just gotten two rooms. Then we also wouldn't have to share a bed like a bunch of college kids on spring break." Nella Rose sounds upbeat, but her chipper tone is thinly veiling what I'm sure is real annoyance. I'm sure she's thinking this trip should have just been the two of them.

"I'd like to think of it more as a sleepover!" Iris chimes in, which I'm grateful for.

I know I should stand my ground and take some hangers, but Nella Rose's comment has made me feel like I'm intruding already.

"It's fine, most of my stuff doesn't need to be hanging anyway," I say as I pull out the knits from my suitcase and avoid letting them see the silk dress that could definitely use a hanger. "I'll take the dresser, no worries!"

"Perfect!" Iris chirps, and the conversation is over.

As I look over my options for the week, I decide to wear my best outfit for tonight in order to gain some confidence. A green tweed skirt with subtle sparkles over black leggings and black suede over-the-knee boots, topped with an ivory sweater that I'll French tuck in the front and let hang over my shoulder. I'll pair it with my black Chanel clutch (a gift from Bennett's mom).

❀

Each dressed on our own take on "New York Night Out," the three of us hop in our Uber and head to dinner, a swanky midtown spot that offered a comp meal in exchange for our promotion (a combined 1.2 million followers on Instagram).

We get seated at a nice table in the middle of the restaurant and order various cutesie cocktails and five items off the starters menu. The girls only nibble on them, but I have to restrain myself from over-indulging. These kinds of dinners are one of the most fun parts about our job, in my opinion. Walking into a restaurant, where they already know you're coming and plan it all out for you like you're some kind of celebrity—it's a really cool feeling.

"So, what do we have to post for this dinner?" Nella Rose says without looking up from her phone.

"Just some stories, no in-feed post," Iris relays to us.

"Iris, we *can* afford to pay for our own dinner, I don't get why you say yes to these comped meals. It's just, like, more work for no reason." Nella Rose takes another sip of her beautiful drink.

Uncomfortable, I resituate myself in my leather seat. I guess it's wrong to like free food? But it was Iris' idea. I decide not to chime in and pretend to be typing something on my phone.

"Oh, come on, it's fun!" says Iris. "Here, let's get a story now." She points her phone at us across the circular table and instructs us to wave and act like we've having fun.

After a few more cocktails, Iris giggles at something Nella Rose says only to her, then turns her attention to me and reaches over to grab my hand across the table, nearly knocking over her rosemary pomegranate martini. She's got to be hammered. She hasn't eaten hardly a thing.

"Sooo how's wedding planning going?! You must be so excited!" Iris beams at me and squeezes my hand tight. She's zeroed in, waiting for my response. This kind of energy she possesses is a skill like no other. I wonder if she's medicated or if it comes naturally.

I smile back, glance over to Nella Rose and see her looking down at her phone. She's not interested.

"Oh it's been so fun," I say. "Bennett is a lifesaver; I don't know how I could ever keep all those contracts and invoices straight."

That's my subtle way of saying he's paying for everything. It's silly, but the feeling of being taken care of like this, especially financially, is really new to me. Having them know this is important to me for some reason.

I'm a first-generation college student with a mountain of student loans waiting to be paid off. My mom immigrated from Mexico at the age of five, and my dad was born into the family of an alcoholic father and neglecting mother. They met while my mom was waitressing at a small diner, and my dad often told me she was the most beautiful woman he had ever seen. They married a month later, love at first sight and all that. College wasn't the top priority on their list.

When I got into Ole Miss, mom cried and dad threw a party and invited everyone we knew.

Now that I have a little money, it feels good to talk about it. Most of it is Bennett's, but I make a decent amount from my blog. Just compared to a doctor's salary it's not that much.

"Well you nabbed yourself a good one!" Iris beams.

I smile in agreement and take a sip of my Moscow mule.

"Virginia, I have to say, why did it take a trip over a thousand miles away for us to all get together?"

Yup, Iris is drunk.

"You tell Bennett that we are having a double date when we get back. I'll have John take off a night; he needs to anyway! That boy, I swear, he works longer hours than any of our boys, and Bennett is a freaking doctor!"

Yes, a future plan. If one double date comes out of this whole trip I'll have considered it a success.

I smile my huge squinty smile at her and agree. "A double date would be so fun! We could always just come over to your place to make it easier for John," I suggest, continuing to smile.

"That's a great idea! I actually have some new barstools I'd love to get your opinion on."

"Oh yeah, I think I saw them on your stories. I'd love to see them in person!"

I steal a glance at Nella Rose as Iris retrieves her hand. Nella Rose is level, but I can tell the subtle way Iris left her out of the double date stung.

Normally, I would have said something like, *only if Nella Rose and Patrick can come!* I absolutely hate leaving people out, but, I mean, it's Nella Rose.

So I don't.

As more food appears on our table, the girls take bites occasionally, but all together it doesn't equal a full meal. I can feel my stomach growling as I force myself to take another sip of my cocktail instead of another bite of the bacon wrapped scallops.

Iris is leaning toward Nella Rose, telling her about something her daughter, Ivory, did last week, when I notice a text message pop up on her phone resting on the table between us. I look at the two of them again to see if Iris is paying attention to me, and when I see she isn't, I take another look at the phone.

The person who texted her isn't saved with a contact—just the 10-digit number is shown—but I immediately recognize it. It's Bennett's number.

At the risk of sounding crazy, I don't say anything to Iris. How can I casually mention that I just happened to see her get a text from my fiancé? As I rationalize it away, I remember my birthday is coming up. Maybe she asked him what to get me for a present?

I'm sure it's nothing.

CHAPTER 8

September 4, 2019

New York, NY

NELLA ROSE

The three of us cram together in a tiny entryway of a coffee shop called Joe's Joe. A little on the nose, don't you think? After waiting thirty minutes—you would think they could have found us a table—we ordered coffee from the bar. I needed that afternoon pick-me-up after all the walking we had been doing.

"Iris!" A hostess yells above the chatting crowd, and we follow her to our table.

Iris sits between us, and she's looking at something Virginia is showing her on her phone. Probably more wedding planning bullshit that we've been listening to nonstop since we arrived. It's like she has nothing else to talk about. It's sorta sad. Marrying a hot doctor is pretty much the best thing happening in her life right now.

I brush out the ends of a piece of hair falling over my shoulder with my fingers. She *was* invited, and I chose to come along knowing she would be here, so I really can't complain too much. I could have avoided this whole thing, but it just happened too fast and I was too afraid of having the trip be cancelled all together. That would have sucked. It's essential to be seen at Fashion Week, and it was way too late to find other roommates.

Also, Iris was already a little mad at me the week the plans were going down. I had hosted a small dinner party for another couple in the neighborhood, and Iris had been pissed that I didn't invite her and her husband. She opened up to me, saying that John was having a hard time making good guy friends, even after six years of living in Mount Pleasant, and that she wanted to basically force him and Patrick to spend time together. I felt bad. That had never occurred to me.

Obviously, I want our husbands to be friends. That would be a good scenario for me, too, it just hadn't occurred to me to try. Patrick is so involved in his own friend group, playing golf every weekend and having regular dinners and happy hours after work so often that he more often than not comes home after I'm already asleep. And he's just so different from John. John is like this…I don't know how to explain it really. I just wouldn't put the two of them together in a room and expect a load of laughs and bro-talk.

But, Iris evidently disagrees and didn't talk to me for two days after she found out about the dinner. I wanted to be annoyed with her for being dramatic, but no one gets annoyed with Iris. She has this way of making you feel like nothing could ever be her fault. It's impressive, really. I wish I had that talent. I tried to make amends, and my efforts all fell on deaf ears until I came to her with the idea of a trip to New York for Fashion Week. She agreed but said she had been talking to Virginia recently and wanted to invite her.

Virginia? What? I remember feeling totally shocked. She hadn't talked about her in forever. They had barely hung out even though she lived just

20 minutes from us in downtown Charleston, and now she wanted to go on a trip with her? Be crammed in a New York hotel suite and share a bathroom with her for three days? I couldn't tell if she was just using this new friendship to make me jealous or if she actually wanted to see her.

Either way, it was a trip for the three of us or no trip at all, so I caved, and here we are.

I take a sip of my latte, take a little breath in, and do what I know I have to in order to make this week bearable.

"What are y'all looking at over there?" I ask as I lean over and pretend to be interested.

"You *have* to see the flower girl dresses Ginny ordered. They're *so* cute I can't even stand it." Iris takes the phone from Virginia and passes it to me.

They are cute, I guess. Little blush ballerina-style dresses with big tulle skirts and tiny floral embroidery on the bodices. Her niece is showing it off in the picture, holding out the skirt and trying to do a big girl pose. She's got to be about four years old, with long brunette hair tied up in a big messy bun on top of her head and brown eyes.

"Aw, this is really cute, Virginia! What's your niece's name again?" As if I care.

"Cynthia. Ah, I know, I miss her so much. Every time I see her, all she talks about is the wedding and how I get to be a princess for the day." Virginia smiles as I hand the phone back to her, and she takes one more look before closing the picture and putting her phone in her little Gucci side bag. That must have been a gift from Bennett. She couldn't afford anything designer on her blog salary. No way. I doubt she brings in six figures, but I guess anyone can have credit card debt.

Her phone screen is cracked, and her boots have scuffs all over them. I realize they're probably last year's. Her manicure is grown out a little, and I saw her put on her sweater this morning with the tag still on it. I'll bet she plans to return a lot of her expensive clothes that she must have bought just for this week to impress us. Oh, the old blogger trick. I never met a girl who didn't do it sometimes, especially when they start out. I tuck a piece of hair behind my ear to expose my diamond earring and hand her the phone back with my left hand to show off my ring.

"So, what's the plan for the day?" Virginia speaks up again. She's gained some confidence from this tiny bit of attention I just gave her. That won't do.

"I say we do drinks at the Plaza before dinner!" I exclaim, and Iris claps her hands together in agreement.

"Oh, yes! That's perfect! Let's go run to the hotel and change." Iris takes a big gulp of her cold brew.

I glance at Virginia and detect the slightest bit of anxiety in her eyes. This trip is racking up more on her AMEX than she was expecting, I'm sure. Poor thing.

CHAPTER 9

September 4, 2019

New York, NY

VIRGINIA

The other two snooze in the bed next to me as I grab for my phone.

4:18 a.m. Shit.

Why does this always happen to me? I'm going to look like hell in the morning. The dim light of my phone stares back at me as I study my photo background, Bennett in a blue suit and bow tie smiling as he dips me back in a red floor-length gown.

After dinner, Nella Rose and I flirted with the idea of going to a bar, but Iris convinced us that we should get an early start tomorrow. She's a married mom of a four-year-old; she's tired of the bar scene, I'm sure.

But then again, Nella Rose also has children.

On our way back to the hotel, we had bumped into another group of bloggers here for Fashion Week, and I instantly recognized them. We were friends online or "Insta-friends," and they had actually invited me to join them for the trip but I had already said yes to Iris. A tall blonde girl named Aynsley wrapped me up in a hug. Not a fake one; a real one.

"Virginia, hey!" Another girl named Amanda said as she hugged me when Aynsley stepped aside. "We didn't think we'd get to see you! Are you having fun?"

"Yes! We missed you at the Pink party!" a third girl, Kaitlyn, said.

"Oh yeah, I totally forgot that was tonight. I'm sad I missed it!" I said. I had forgotten completely.

"Oh, um, Aynsley, Amanda, Kaitlyn, this is Iris and Nella Rose." I introduced the two groups.

Iris enthusiastically greeted them, and Nella Rose followed suit with a bit less energy.

I turned to say something to Kaitlyn, but she had focused all her energy on Iris and Nella Rose, obviously recognizing them from Instagram. While these three girls had great pages, they're more on my level. Kaitlyn, I learned in this moment, was also a coattail chaser, totally forgetting about her two friends standing behind her. I turned toward Amanda and Aynsley to chat.

"Oh, sorry our Uber is here." Nella Rose turned toward the street without a goodbye to the other girls.

"It was so nice to meet y'all, and I'll get your handles from Virginia so I can follow back!" Iris smiled and followed Nella Rose into the backseat of the car.

I gave the girls a quick hug and we said our goodbyes as well.

As we rode together to the hotel, I started to think about how different this trip would be if I were on it with nice girls like Aynsley and Amanda. I bet they would have given me room in the closet. And could Nella Rose have been any more of a snob? I thought she would lean over and say a snarky remark about the girls to Iris, but then I remembered that's not the blogger way. No talking crap; that's the rule. You never know who you'll be seated next to at an event or grouped with for a trip. Or, heaven forbid, who might end up eclipsing you with followers one day.

No, Nella Rose had been around long enough to know how it goes.

We got into bed at about midnight, and I've probably slept twenty minutes. I have too many thoughts in my head.

I had watched her carefully the rest of the night, but I never saw Iris answer the text from Bennett. When she had picked up her phone to take a boomerang with me for her Instagram, she just swiped away from the text as if it was nothing. Every time she got on her phone the rest of the evening, it didn't look like she was texting, except one time when she got a text from her husband, John, who had sent her a photo of Ivory playing on her jungle gym in the backyard.

Am I crazy?

Is it possible I read the number wrong?

Could it have been someone with a really similar number? It's just that Bennett is from Tennessee, so he's the only person I know of that would have that area code. I shake my head and try to just forget about it. I'm sure it's nothing.

I set my phone carefully on the bedside table and rub my eyes gently. I roll over in the soft hotel sheets and try to find sleep, but I can tell it's no use. Looking over to the window I remember there's a balcony with a view. The sparkling lights of the city call me to come look. I've always loved a good view.

I creep toward the closet and find my Neverfull and unzip my laptop from its case. I've been working on my novel for two years. It's definitely taken a backseat to my blog and my life in general. It's not really part of my plan. I've slowly but surely added pages to my draft over time, and lately the time or inspiration to write just hasn't been there. I clutch the cool metal in my hands and tiptoe to the balcony door.

"Mmmmm." The cold hits my face and I watch my icy breath dance around in the soft breeze. This is nice. I quietly slide the door behind me and wrap a blanket snugly over my shoulders. I'm already wearing socks and a long-sleeve and pants pajama set, so it's pretty comfortable out here for September in New York City.

I stare out into the night as I lean my weight against the railing. Fifteen stories below drunk party goers are making their way home to their hotels. Two girls stumble by as they discuss a creep they dodged at the bar. A bachelor party whoops and hollers as they play-shove each other's shoulders. A couple stops in an alley to make out against a dirty brick wall.

I watch the icy clouds of my breath go out in a puff then slowly disintegrate into the night. Out of sight.

Puff…simmer… puff…simmer…

What a life that would be, to be like my breath in the air. To live in one instant of beauty and glory, then quickly fall away. Disappear. No worries about tomorrow. Too beautiful and sparkly to care.

It's the future that's scary, not the now.

What if this trip is all for nothing?

My nails click away on the keyboard as the words come to me. If I were to ever let anyone read this, they would probably think I have some serious issues, but I don't think that's really the case. I just don't have the talent of letting the realities of the world roll off my back as if they're nothing.

The difficult things in life are what inspire me to find the beauty in it, and this day has been difficult. Now, I not only have the stress of trying to keep up this façade in front of Iris and Nella Rose, I have the text to worry about too.

CHAPTER 10

March 9, 2020

Mount Pleasant, SC

NELLA ROSE

Holding my favorite coffee mug, a souvenir from our family trip to Nashville, I stare into the backyard, scattered with evidence of little girls—a hot pink child-sized trampoline, baby dolls, a tiny tricycle, little purple sandals by the door. I haven't seen our babies for two days, and I'm starting to ache for them. Mom insisted on watching them for the whole weekend to keep them away from all the chaos. Normally I can't wait to get them out of the house, but two days is a long time without them, and now even I am feeling some motherly affection.

Our oldest, Corinne, is four. She's our china doll baby. She's going to be beautiful, which is important. If she gets my nose, which we won't know if she will for years, we'll just take care of it in high school. She also has a confident and bossy personality.

"No one will ever take advantage of this girl," Patrick always says, and I agree. She'll be able to handle herself.

Her shiny "bronde" hair sits at her shoulders from a kitchen scissor accident. I wore sunglasses in the salon as they chopped off her gorgeous locks, trying to hide the tears. She has huge blue eyes and perfectly-placed dimples in her cheeks. You're not supposed to favor them, but she's my first and she looks like me. I sometimes can't help myself.

Eleanor is our little squish. At two years old, her cheeks are still round and puffy like they were when she was a chubby infant, and her dark brown eyes contrast beautifully with her platinum blonde hair. One squinty smile from her and all is forgiven, even after her most terrible tantrums.

I watch our housekeeper go around and tidy up all the little girl things before the remembrance. The "remembrance" for Iris that I'm hosting starts at 10:00 a.m.. I look over at the clock on the microwave—7:25—Patrick will be rolling out of bed in about an hour. He always sleeps in on weekends, and he'll definitely have a golf game with his friends that will start sometime before the girls get here. Still, I'll make sure and wake him up at 8:30 by "accident," AKA making a smoothie or opening a door so the chime of the alarm goes off. He'll come downstairs pretending he's been up for hours and condescendingly ask what I've been doing with my morning. Why is waking up first in the morning always such a competition? What's wrong with sleeping in?

I take my empty mug over to the coffee maker to pour another cup. My morning coffee has become a ritual, always with a plentiful dollop of sweet flavored creamer and maybe a drop of whiskey. It's a time for me to collect myself before the craziness. On weekdays, I always wake the girls up around 6:00 a.m. for daycare, and until they leave with the nanny around 7:30 it's a madhouse. It's a blur of waffles, socks, backpacks, lunchboxes, bows, Goldfish, dresses, and sneakers. As soon as the door shuts behind Amber, the nanny, usually holding a still-sleepy Eleanor and probably chasing Corinne down the walkway, and Patrick drives away to work after a quick peck on the cheek, I go for my coffee, my silk robe sweeping around my pedicured feet as I walk across the wood floor.

We have a gorgeous view of the marsh from the sunroom, which is where you'll find me perched for the next two to three hours once I'm alone. I've been doing this since we moved into this house. I scroll my feed, answer emails, plan my posts, write a little, but mostly I'm just reveling in this alone time. It seems like forever since I started my blog. Really it feels like a lifetime ago, but to be exact, it was about six years ago.

Before the babies, before Patrick, before the sunroom with a view, I was living in my tiny one-bedroom apartment in West Ashley, another Charleston neighborhood. I had been blogging for about four months. I came across her from a quick search of the Carolina bloggers. She had stopped me in my tracks.

Iris Sutten. Her blog name was @iamiriss—a lucky grab with all the active users out there—but after a bit of research I realized she had been at this for a while. I scrolled through the archives on her website and found its start date of almost a year earlier. She was way ahead of me, and her numbers showed it. She had 280,000 followers on Instagram and was averaging 10,000 likes per photo. Right on par for her following and very impressive. I realized I was already so very behind.

I had considered myself to be pretty impressive at the time with 15,000 followers, my handle now @nellarosemiller, which I changed it to after Patrick and I got married, but I was brought down to earth by this bright and beautiful face staring back at me from Iris's page.

She was stunning, tall, with super-long hair with the help of flawless honey blonde extensions. She had big green eyes, freckled cheeks, and a perfect button nose. I felt envious as I touched the tip of my own too-big nose. The kind of girl who is obviously going to get Insta-famous, it was just bound to happen. I spent hours scrolling through her feed, reading every caption, noticing every detail of her life. She was dating someone named John, an incredibly handsome finance guy. They met in college, and instead of taking a job in New York where he could have made three times his current salary, he moved to Charleston to be with Iris because her family was from there. They were close to getting engaged;you could just tell that sort of thing by how confident a girl got with her social posts.

I put my phone down that day and realized I had sat there for almost six hours looking through her blog and Instagram. I adjusted my aching knees and stood up to get more coffee. I remember feeling this awful sensation. Was it jealousy, just as simple as that? I wasn't sure, but I knew this life I was living wasn't measuring up to Iris'.

There were so many things about my life that I wanted to change, bigger things than just getting a nose job. I had been watching girls like Iris on social media for years, yearning for the perfect life. The beautiful girls with the seemingly endless pockets who had everything they could possibly want. I looked around my apartment the day I saw Iris for the first time and realized more than ever how unhappy I was with my current life.

Things needed to happen. I needed to take some action if things were going to change.

I had been planning on breaking up with my current boyfriend after our last nasty fight, but instead I walked over to my couch and picked up my phone. I opened my text messages and started typing.

"Hey Patrick, are we still on for tomorrow?"

The first step to making my life the way I wanted it to be was the perfect rich husband, and Patrick at least had the rich part down. Now it's been six years, and I have all the boxes I had been looking for checked off.

Most expensive piece of real estate in the city, check. Nose job, check. Handsome husband, check. Beautiful children, check. Envious life, check.

No one here knew me before I was with Patrick. The fancy gifts rolled in right away. I know it stroked his ego to show off what kind of life he could give me, and I never opposed any of it. After six months of dating, he gave me my Range Rover. I pulled up to Iris' house for our first hangout in it. She never knew my humble beginnings, and just a little white lie here and there was all it took to keep my secret.

CHAPTER 11

September 4, 2019

New York, NY

VIRGINIA

I must have dozed off.

The cushy balcony sofa made for a more comforting bed than the luxe and empty queen in the room, and that sleeping pill was a godsend. I blink at the rays from the orange sunrise beaming on my face and decide I should get back inside before the girls see my empty bed and worry.

I carefully slide open the door, expecting to find them still sleeping, but their bed is empty as well, and I can hear their indistinct chatter coming from the bathroom. They're up and getting ready.

Didn't they wonder where I was? Why didn't they come check on me?

Too stung to put on a face and greet them in the bathroom, I roll into my own bed and check my phone. Lots of notifications. People are excited that I'm here.

With them.

I do a little happy dance on the inside as I feel the sweet wave of approval rush over me.

206 new followers.

5,762 likes and 407 comments on my post from dinner last night.

One tagged photo of me from Iris' post.

I set my phone down and my heart sings. I close my eyes and can't help but smile.

Then reality sets in. I need to know why they're up so early. It's 7:00 a.m.. Maybe they made plans I need to know about. I swallow my pride and peek into the doorway.

"Morning, y'all." I do my best to sound tired but cheery.

"Oh hey! You looked so peaceful out there we didn't want to disturb you," Iris chirps. "You've got plenty of time to get ready; we don't leave for breakfast for another hour." She flips her beautiful blonde locks over her shoulder as she applies more under eye concealer.

Still, I'm missing the girl time. I try not to look visibly hurt. *Smiles, Virginia, smiles,* I remind myself.

I smile. "Oh yes! I can't wait, this place is supposed to be so cute. I think it has a frose bar."

"If you have anything pink, that'd be so cute for a picture. Come see!" Iris passes me in the doorway to show me what she and Nella Rose have hung in the closet next to each other. Two perfectly coordinated outfits, both with a pink wool pea coat. Almost identical coats, really. They had to have planned that.

I didn't bring a pink pea coat.

"SO cute!" I rave as I rack my brain thinking of the collection of clothes I packed that could match theirs.

The happy feelings have completely disappeared.

Puff…simmer…

CHAPTER 12

March 9, 2020

Mount Pleasant, SC

NELLA ROSE

I drain the last drop of coffee, the splash of whiskey was necessary this morning, and snap back to the present in my beautiful sunroom. I've got to get the house perfect before the other girls arrive.

Opening both French doors, I walk around the back deck. It's a warm spring day in Mount Pleasant, and the early morning sun is sparkling off the water in the harbor at the end of our dock. Steps from our patio lead to our 2.1-acre backyard—plenty of room for a lawn and vegetable garden, our symmetrical and stylish rectangle pool, four mature oak trees, and two magnolia trees. We have a small wooden fence separating our backyard from the marsh for the safety of the kids; you never know when a curious alligator might creep into your yard around here. A

100-yard wooden dock sits right in the middle of the fence leading out to the harbor where we store our two boats, a dusty blue Freeman 42LR for fishing and a black Scout 330 LXF with light leather interior for joyrides with our friends.

My mind starts to blank as I take it in. It's what I do to remind myself that this kind of thing costs something. It doesn't happen for free. Scooping up a few dolls and baby shoes that the cleaners missed, I move back inside to pretend like I'm cleaning the kitchen before I can go upstairs and start getting myself ready for the day.

"Rosie, have you seen my blue golf shorts?!" Patrick's low voice hollers from the foyer louder than necessary.

"In the laundry room!"

I hear him rummaging around looking for them as I remember I was supposed to do a load before today. Shit.

"They're still in the hamper! I told you I needed these today!"

Deep breaths. My eyes squeeze closed as tight as my clenched left hand fist for a brief second as I prepare myself.

"I have a tournament today, and this is what we're wearing. What am I supposed to do now?" His voice is low, not yelling, but I can tell this could get worse if I don't play it right.

He stares at me and continues, "Do I need to add laundry to the list of the crap I do for this family? I don't mind, you just need to tell me so this doesn't keep happening. I don't think it's too much to ask that you do a few things around the house in your spare time while I'm busy working my ass off."

I cannot believe he's doing the whole tired speech after everything happening right now. Is this the most important thing in our lives right now? I don't have the strength to get into it with him right now.

"You're right, I'm sorry." My tone is well-rehearsed, like an experienced actress doing her last performance of the season. I wish it would be my last time on stage in this role, but lately that doesn't seem like that will ever be the case.

"Right." He looks me over. He's been studying me more than normal lately. "I think I know where another pair is." And with that he turns and leaves me in the kitchen. I exhale deeply in relief and turn back to the sink.

As much as I try to stop them, I blink a few tears from my eyes, then wipe them away quickly and try to think of something else.

If I thought I could handle Corinne and Eleanor by myself I would pick up the phone right now and fire the nanny, but the thought of jelly on the white rug of my home office and having my mornings in the sunroom taken away from me pushes the thought out of my head. I can take a few comments like this from Patrick in exchange for my lovely days at home alone. My view, my oak trees, my designer bags, my sunroom.

I wipe my face again and move to the sink to put away the hand-washed dishes. I carefully dry the blue plate with a yellow seersucker dish towel and place it on the marble waterfall counter with a clink. I grab for a crystal Tiffany serving bowl and gently rinse the chicken salad residue. Remaining in the sink for me to wash next are my Puiforcat flatware, my gold Haviland tea cups with matching saucers, and my Shun Kaji set of knives.

All my beautiful things.

CHAPTER 13

September 6, 2019

New York, NY

VIRGINIA

How did all of this fit? I wonder as I try to repack my suitcases with all my clothes from the trip. I only bought one scarf and one sweater (both returnable, even though Bennett will insist that I keep them), and yet the zippers on my suitcases are bursting at the seams like my jeans on Friday pizza cheat night.

It seems like we just got here, and we are already getting ready to leave our fabulous hotel to go back to reality down South. Same airport and arrival days, and yet flights weren't coordinated between the three of us. I'm on the 1:45 p.m. while Iris and Nella Rose will take the 3:30 p.m..

I'm Sorry!! Nella Rose had texted me after I told her about the flight deal I had found. *We are so loyal to our airline, Patrick would kill me if I didn't get those points!*

I thought to myself, *You failed to mention that allegiance in other texts about the flights, and since when does someone with more money than God need to worry about points*?

Instead I answered, *OH girl you gotta get those points, I'll see y'all in NY!*

Iris hadn't responded to any of my texts about the trip. Nella Rose claimed she was terrible at texting and it would be easier for the two of us to work out the details. I agreed; she is a really busy woman. I can't imagine how many texts she must get a day. But still, Iris was the one who invited me, so it was so weird when I was only talking details with Nella Rose.

Really weird.

I push down on top of the hard silver shell with all my strength and finally zip up the last suitcase. I stand up, my knees cracking from squatting too long, and lift the suitcase upright by its leather handle and roll it next to the rest of its matching set by the door.

I grab my phone from the doorside table; it's placed next to an extravagant floral arrangement. Pink lilies, blush dahlias, magenta roses, lavender irises, and white gypsophila with a note from the PR company who had set up our stay. *Enjoy your girls' trip!* it read in happy, swirly cursive letters.

I reach out and gently rub one of the velvety petals between my fingers and note the inclusion of irises and roses.

My middle name is also Rose, but I never include it on anything. It had been a thought in the back of my mind when I changed my blog name a few years ago, but I knew I'd look like I was trying to force my way into their *club.*

The Flower Girls.

That's what they called themselves. Iris and Nella Rose came up with it after becoming friends for two seconds and it stuck. I see why; it's really catchy, but still kind of stupid. Right? In any case, anything they did together was always labeled with the name, and now when anyone talks about the two of them, they're referred to as *The Flower Girls.*

The Flower Girls grabbing a cupcake at Sweets Shop.

The Flower Girls shopping at their favorite local boutique.

The Flower Girls are taking a trip to New York! read a caption from Nella Rose's page the day before we left. In the photo, she and Iris are beaming at each other through matching sunglasses on the steps of Nella Rose's house. I know it's hers because I know what both of their houses look like in detail from their posts.

"Can't wait to spend three whole days with this beauty!"

22,254 likes and 450 comments.

I can't wait to see you and @meetvirginialane <3, Iris had commented.

At least Iris remembers I'm coming, I had thought as I saw how she included me when Nella Rose hadn't. I convinced myself she hadn't added me in because a current photo of the three of us didn't exist, but after these past three days with her I'm not so sure.

I'm really trying not to be too sensitive, but I couldn't help but notice Nella Rose leaving me out every chance that she got. I was usually the one taking photos of the two of them together while Iris sweetly offered to take my solo shots. Nella Rose never offered to take photos of me and Iris, and twice when Iris and I had asked for her to take our photo, she had diverted the conversation, saying it was freezing and we'd get it later or we didn't want to miss our reservations.

I left the trip with six solo outfit shots, one group shot of the three of us we got at dinner, and one shot of me and Iris. I'd really been hoping for more. If she'd liked how she looked in any photos of the two of us, she would have posted them, too, giving me more exposure.

"I guess I'd better head down," I say in my Virginia-chipper tone, and Iris pops her head out from the bathroom holding her curling iron, half her hair pinned up on one side, the other draping down over her left shoulder with fresh, bouncy curls.

"Oh no! Is it time already?! Aw, Ginny this trip went by *way* too fast!" She disappears back in the bathroom to set down the hot iron and runs out to embrace me.

"I know, I'm so sad to leave! But let's go on that double date we talked about! I'll text you when I know Bennett's schedule next week." I smile and hug her back. Nella Rose has yet to make her appearance.

"I'm heading out, Nella Rose!" I say to the open door. Do I go in there, or wait for her to come out?

It feels like a power battle. The upper hand going to the person who doesn't go out of her way to approach the other.

Before I can decide she struts out looking 100% photoshoot ready. I can't believe the perfection of her curls, and she bats her long eyelashes at me and fingers a diamond stud earring.

She is sparkling.

I feel bad even thinking this, but even with all that makeup, you can tell she's not exactly a natural beauty. She's lucky contouring became a thing when it did. She's had a nose job, but it's still not just right. Her eyes are a little too close together. But, she's as skinny as Iris and probably even weighs ten pounds less with their height difference, and that's all that matters in our world, really. "This was so fun. Let's do it again soon."

An empty promise, I can tell.

She calmly smiles but instead of hugging me, she avoids my eyes and looks over to my suitcases. I can see her looking at the smudges and small dents from checking them. Like there's anything I could do about that, but I can see the judgement in her eyes. She looks back at me and keeps her close-mouthed smile.

I retreat to the door as I hear the knock of the bellman here to help me with my suitcases. Time to go.

Iris walks me to the door and Nella Rose stays in her place, gives me a small wave and returns to the bathroom. I welcome the moment alone with Iris. Maybe she'll mention the text.

With one more hug and kiss on the cheek, Iris says in my ear, "Don't worry about Nella Rose. She's just jelly because I knew you first."

"Ha, I get it. No worries, I had a great time!"

❀

I wave down Bennett at the Charleston International Airport as he pulls up to get me. It may not have that many outgoing flight options—we only have gates A and B, and most of our flights require a layover in Charlotte—but I love it. It's so small and clean and quaint, with easy pickup and dropoff, and great food.

The big tires of his truck come to a halt in front of me, and he steps down and walks around the front to greet me.

"Hey, stranger!" Bennett wraps me up in a tight bear hug that lifts me from the ground for a second.

"Hey, babe! I missed you," I say as he sets me back down.

"I missed you too!" he says and grabs my luggage to throw it in the back of the truck. I open the door and grab the handle to help myself up into my shotgun seat.

As we ride down the road, he asks me a few questions about the trip, treading lightly as usual, and I answer, but I still can't stop thinking about the text to Iris while we were at dinner. I had almost asked him last night, but I thought better of it and decided to wait until I could ask in person so I could see how he reacted and decide if he was being truthful.

It's way too easy to lie in a text, with plenty of time to plan out what you're going to say.

I guess he can sense that something's on my mind.

"Virginia, what happened? I can tell something's wrong with you," he says, keeping his eyes on the road so as not to pressure me too much. This is his way of getting things out of me. He thinks that if he acts nonchalant that I'll feel more obliged to open up to him. I'm not sure where he learned this, but it's interesting to see. He only does it when he thinks he's asking something loaded.

"Well, I wasn't going to say anything, but yeah, something has been on my mind. I, um, saw Iris get a text from you." I look his way. He looks calm and ready to answer, but lets me finish. "I didn't think it was a big deal, but then Iris never brought it up to me. So, I just wanted to know what it was about." Inside I'm shaking, waiting for the worst.

"Babe, that was about your *surprise* birthday dinner!" He smiles and reaches for his phone in the middle console and tosses it on my lap playfully. "Go ahead, read them. The secret is out now anyway." He lets out a small chuckle and reaches over to put a hand on my knee. "Come on, what did you think it was?"

In a stronger moment I might have said, "Oh no, I trust you, I don't need to check," but I type in his passcode and open messages to find their texts. There they are. The most innocent and appropriate text exchange, chatting about where we should go for my birthday dinner and whether I wanted yellow or rose gold for a necklace she was getting me.

A sigh of relief exits my body, and all the twists in my stomach ring themselves out. I could handle the stress of the comparison game from the NY trip, but I can't handle anything going wrong with the two people in this truck.

But I can't help but think that it's odd how she's already feeling so close to me. Close enough to buy me a birthday gift? I felt like this week went well enough, but they were texting on the first day of the trip. Why is she suddenly trying to be my friend?

Obviously, this was the goal, and I should be happy about it, but I somehow can't accept it. Still, I'm at least relieved for now that things are fine with Bennett and nothing weird went on there.

"Sorry about that, I didn't mean to ruin the surprise," I say as I exchange the phone in my hand for his hand and hold it tightly.

"It's okay. I'm sure that would have freaked me out if I were in your place." We roll up to a stop sign, and he leans over to give me a kiss across the large console. I have to lift myself up off the seat a bit to reach his lips, and I smile as I set myself back down.

CHAPTER 14

March 9, 2020

Mount Pleasant, SC

NELLA ROSE

Patrick has left for his golf tournament. No goodbye today, and was he carrying another bag other than his golf bag? I straighten up the dishes on the bone white linen tablecloth. I have the perfect shape and size dish for each food item, all matching, of course, along with the most gorgeous crystal punch bowl with dainty matching cups. I made a lemon and mint punch from Patrick's mother's recipe book she gave me as a wedding gift. The two waitresses I hired are placing appetizers on trays and spooning servings of punch in the cups to pass around to the guests when they arrive.

The girls will be here any minute, so I walk to the guest bath and check my appearance one more time. I want to see if I look okay for the girls, but I also just want to admire myself a little. I haven't eaten much in the past three weeks, and I look better than I did before the girls were born.

In the large mirror my reflection stares back at me. I frown. She's not right for this occasion. Should I smear my makeup to look like I was crying? Or, maybe wear something a little more casual? I've decided on a cotton black maxi day dress. It has thin straps that come together in small bows on top of my shoulders with a tapered waist that shows off my figure and a subtle pleated skirt. I don't know, though, the bows seem too happy. I frown again.

I consider running upstairs to change into my black linen shift dress when the doorbell rings. It's too late; this will have to do, I suppose. I gently rub beneath my eyes to imperfect my mascara and squeeze my eyes shut tight for a few seconds to give them a watery appearance, and as I make my way toward the door to answer, I wonder who will arrive first.

❀

VIRGINIA

This is insane.

I'm spellbound as I drive the winding streets toward Nella Rose's "house" in my little SUV. I've seen it before once or twice, but I've never been invited inside. To be honest, I wasn't sure I'd even get an invitation today, but I guess she thought it would look weird to invite all the local bloggers and exclude me.

Weird and rude.

No, it would make Nella Rose look terrible if she left me out. All the girls in town knew we were "friends" after they saw us together at Fashion Week last fall. Everything that's happened since then could never be traced back to Iris or Nella Rose.

They were smarter than that.

As well as I thought that week had gone, the month after New York everything changed. Iris and Nella Rose had been spending every moment together, leaving me out. It was too much for me to handle, watching them pop up on my feed together, rubbing in my face how much fun they were having.

Then, it got worse.

"Baby, it's okay, you have other friends. Why do you care so much about being included?" Bennett had held my head against his chest and stroked my hair as I sobbed.

I'd sat up and pushed him off, and stared into his dark worried eyes.

"It's about more than that, Bennett. I know it's hard to explain to someone who's not in this world, but when you're successful, no one leaves you out. Everyone wants to be around you because you'll all benefit each other's successes. It's just how it is. So, them leaving me out means more than them just not liking me, which I can handle, because why would I want to be liked by someone like Nella Rose? No, it means I'm irrelevant to them. I'm not good enough for them to need anything from me."

A car horn blares behind me and snaps me back to Plantation Meadows. I'm sitting at a stop sign completely zoned out. I might have overdone the meds today; I'm a little loopy. As I continue to pull up toward her house, I can't help my thoughts and I drift again.

I start to think more about them.

In late September, we had run into each other at Trader Joe's on a random Wednesday. Iris couldn't have been nicer, and we'd decided to stop our grocery shopping and buy some wine for a girls' night at her place. Just me and her.

Make her like me.

We'd sat on her sofa in their sitting room (John must be some sweet guy for not caring about having a pink sofa) and drank rosé. We talked about everything under the sun, even the good old days, which I thought she had forgotten. I was amazed to hear her talk about her husband. She had always portrayed John as this perfect guy on her page, but it was weird seeing them interact in person. He was doting, but she was a bit dismissive. Not to the point where it was obvious or rude, but something was just off.

We had fun though. She even put me on her Instagram stories that night. A selfie snap of us cheers-ing with our glasses along with the text *Girl's night with my Ginny @meetvirginialane.*

I got 478 new followers.

I make the turn into Nella Rose's driveway, and as I drive up to her gigantic (no word seems right, maybe colossal is more accurate) Southern-style home through its iron entrance gates, I realize that I'm the first to arrive based on the empty circle drive.

The house is all white with pale blue shutters and a matching blue double farm-style door, three stories, nestled in the most expensive area you can buy in this town. It has large porches that span the entire length of the house on each floor and a double staircase that leads to the entry. She has a big enough yard and space between her house and her neighbors for me to see the end of a dock that leads out to the harbor.

A mansion on the water. You couldn't dream up a more perfect Southern home if you tried. It's like the one Noah builds Allie in *The Notebook.*

It's not too late; I can leave right now. But I remember why I'm here.

Iris.

How quickly things had shifted between us.

Would Iris be happy knowing I was here celebrating her memory? Would she think me pathetic for even showing up after everything?

It's too late to back out now. I'd better go inside before Nella Rose sees me sitting out here in my car. I look like an idiot waiting for someone else to get there so I'm not the first one in.

I check myself in the rearview mirror. Will they be able to see through me?

Whether I'm ready or not, I have to face them.

Don't be a coward, I say to myself.

CHAPTER 15

September 30, 2019

Mount Pleasant, SC

NELLA ROSE

Everywhere I look all I see is *fucking Virginia.* I guess she and Iris had such a blast together when we were in New York because now she always wants to invite *Virginia* to everything we do. Stuff that was just our thing is becoming a threesome, and I am not about it. And now they're hanging out, just the two of them, *without me?*

I glare at my phone, willing it to light up with a text from Iris saying how Virginia forced her way over to her house, how she's having a terrible time with her, but it's no use. I can see it on her face in that stupid selfie. Iris is having fun with *her.*

"UGHH!!" I throw my phone and it lands with a thud on the chaise lounge across the room from me.

I march myself to the kitchen for another whiskey sour with lime from the bar cart.

I set the glass down and add three cubes of ice from the ice bucket. They make a satisfying clink as they hit the bottom of the crystal. I rack my brain as I serve myself a generous pour of Westland Garryana. Did Iris think I was out of town? Maybe she thought I had Corinne's dance recital tonight. No, of course not, Ivory is in the same class. Maybe she thought I was having date night with Patrick? There must be something, I have to check.

I forget to add the sour and walk back into the sitting room, glass in hand to retrieve my phone. I go through my posts from today to see why she would have thought I couldn't make it to girls' night. I scroll through my posts but see nothing that makes me look too unavailable. I check my texts again and nothing.

That hateful bitch. She's trying to take Iris away from me. I'll bet Iris tried to invite me but Virginia told her not to. "Let's just keep it to you and me tonight!" I can hear her stupid voice saying as Iris starts a text to me but deletes it.

"On the rocks again, Rosie?" I jump at the sound of Patrick's voice and my crystal glass slips from my hand and crashes to the wood floor, shattering in a million sparkling diamonds.

"Ah!" I yelp as I quickly draw my feet under me to avoid the shards.

"*Really?* Calm the fuck down; it's just me!" He's thrown down his briefcase and slapped a hand over his face in exasperation.

"I'm sorry, you just scared me. I was zoned out. I didn't realize the…" I'm shaking a little from the commotion and the loud sound of the glass breaking. He stands there just looking at me.

"I'm going to go shower." He stares at me for a second, daring me to ask his help or get upset at him for yelling, then turns and ascends the stairs out of sight.

I can't help the tears now. They pour down my face as I sob into a blue embroidered throw pillow. Tiny golden birds and green ivy dance across the soft silk fabric. I withdraw my face to take a closer look and realize I've left a mascara smudge on one of the birds. It's barely noticeable, but I'll get the stain remover anyway after I clean up the glass.

I slowly push myself up and look around our perfect sunroom.

The abstract painting of Sullivan's Island at sunset on the wall costs $4,000. I could buy several brand new five bedroom homes in West Ashley if I sold just the jewelry I was wearing right now (my diamond stud earrings, my engagement ring, my wedding band and my tennis bracelet.) The pour of whiskey in my glass that I'm casually drinking on a weekday would set me back $50 at a bar. The crystal I just broke is an antique and irreplaceable.

I wipe my face, check my phone one more time, then tip toe across the room to retrieve the broom Patrick so sweetly left out for me.

CHAPTER 16

March 9, 2020

Mount Pleasant, SC

NELLA ROSE

"I can't *believe* they're trying to make you a suspect, Nella!" Mary's shrill voice echoes as we sit in the sunroom.

Nella *Rose*, I think to myself, but I won't correct the poor girl.

"I know, it's insane. She was my best friend. Like, why on earth would I ever want to hurt my closest friend?" All the girls look to me and murmur their own agreements. I've carefully thought out my answers to all the obvious questions that were sure to come my way. Our lawyer had advised me not to have this event until they had found a solid suspect, but I couldn't put this off. All eyes are on me to be the supportive mourning best friend.

I take a small sip of the punch and return it to the side table next to my seat on the sofa. I glance over at Virginia, sitting as far away from me as possible across the room. She looks good, which is irritating. Her choice of dress is much more appropriate for the occasion, and I curse myself again for wearing this stupid bow dress. I'm still thinner than her, though, by a lot. She's nibbling on one of the tea sandwiches I made, despite herself.

"I just wish I could have gotten to know her better." Sydney wipes away a tear with an embroidered *M* napkin, one of the wedding gifts from my sister. "She seemed like such a sweet girl. She always wrote the nicest comments. I would have liked to have met her in person." She appears really genuine as she continues to dab her cheeks, not even trying to keep from messing up her makeup. What a mess this girl is.

I look around and realize something. Virginia and I are the only girls in this room of eleven bloggers who have met her in person. It's no surprise how they can all feel this connected to her just through her presence online.

"So, why is it that you're a suspect, Nella Rose? I don't get it!" Ann asks from her spot next to me on the sofa as she holds a cup of tea gently in her lap on top of her black and white polka dot skirt. This girl is something else. She messages me on Instagram a couple times a week saying things like *we should get drinks sometime!* or *you should come to our blogger event*! or *I would love to meet you sometime!* What a fake. Her efforts are transparent, but I decided to invite all the blogger girls I knew of in the area because I didn't want to be rude. Of course she snagged the spot next to me right away.

"It's crazy, honestly. Patrick and I pay $250 a month for a top of the line security system and it decides to break two days before her murder. There's no footage stored from that night at all. I have no alibi because I was here at home, but there's no way to prove it. It's literally insane." I've told this story about 50 times the past week. I like having the attention of the room, though, so I go on.

"Also, I was the last one to see her. We had happy hour that evening at The Watch, and with John being out of town and Ivory at her sister's house, there's no one to say where she was after that. I don't know, though, I'm not really worried. I'm sure they'll find some evidence that will clear my name, they're just guessing at this point."

"Can't they trace where your phone was?" Lauren chimes in.

"Not really. You can trace where phones are currently but not where they were unless you made calls or sent texts. I sent one text to Patrick around 8:00 p.m.. Since they found her the next morning around 5:00 a.m.—I think it was by a jogger in the neighborhood—that doesn't prove anything. It's morbid to say, but she was still warm when they found her. I've been told they think she was killed around 4:00 to 5:00 a.m., and she was strangled, so there's no murder weapon." Do I sound too okay again? Having all their eyes on me has distracted me from my role.

"It's just so hard to be questioned like this when I'm still in mourning over losing like my dearest friend. They have no sympathy for what I'm going through at all." Yes, I got a tear to drop and gingerly dab it away.

"I can't imagine what John is going through."

I snap my head up at the sound of her voice. Virginia has finally decided to say something, and of course it's something to cut down my feelings and bring attention to someone else. Why is she even here? I dig my nails into my palm as I squeeze the napkin in my lap.

All the girls chirp in agreement about how horribly misfortunate it is to leave John and Ivory without a wife and mother. They start discussing the meals and gifts they can bring them and then Mary turns to me. "Have you gone by to see them yet, Nella?"

All eyes on me.

I take another sip of my punch to give myself a moment to prepare. What's the right thing to say here? The truth is, I haven't made it over there yet. With all the police and detectives and questions and shopping for black mourning outfits, I just haven't found the time. Also, I can't stand the thought of seeing little Ivory.

"No, I haven't yet. I thought it would be best to give them space. I'm sure they have crowds of people coming to see them every day. I don't want to add more stress." That sounded okay, and it was partly true. All the girls murmur their agreement.

"Oh no, I feel bad now! I stopped by to bring them a casserole. Maybe that wasn't the right thing to do, I just wanted to check on them."

I keep my eyes focused on my punch glass.

Really?! YOU went by to see them, Virginia? You don't even *know* them that well, you psycho. Why would they possibly want you there bothering them? And now you're rubbing in my face what a good friend you are to her even after death by comforting her family?

I could snap right here if I don't watch myself. I let out the breath I've been holding.

Slowly I look up and catch her eyes from across the room. No one is looking at me, it's all eyes on her with reassurance that it was a nice thing to do, but she's staring back at me. She's waiting for me to say something. She knows I look like a fool and a shitty friend to Iris. I set down my cup to keep from throwing it in her stupid doe-eyed face.

I breathe, "No, I'm sure they really appreciated that."

❀

As I excuse the waitresses and say goodbye to the guests, I turn back into the house to find Virginia still there. She's putting some cups in the sink.

"Virginia, really, you don't have to do that. The housekeeper will be here in an hour. I'm sure you're exhausted. You should go home." Doesn't she get the hint? *Get out!*

She looks up from the sink at me standing across from her at my marble kitchen island with a strange expression on her face.

"Look, I've been wanting to talk to you about this for a while. I know it's weird timing, but still." She's now fumbling with her watch, a rose gold Michele with diamonds around the face, which must have been a gift from Bennett. I move my eyes from her wrist back to meet hers again.

"I feel like there's something I should tell you. Something…about Iris," she says nervously.

There's no way I'm going to let her say this. There's no reason for this to get out, especially now that Iris is gone. It would just be something she'd be able to hang over my head. "She…"

No, I will not let her have this.

I interrupt her with a wave in her direction. "There's no reason to tell me anything about Iris right now. That is so disrespectful, Virginia. Whatever you think you need to say, just save it, okay?" I grab her purse sitting on my barstool and walk toward the front door. "I think it's time for you to leave my house."

I hear her footsteps follow behind me but I keep my back to her until I reach the door.

"Goodbye, Virginia." I say. It has a period at the end. I hope this is the last time I have to speak to her.

She walks through the doorway, but turns around to face me before I have a chance to close the door.

"I guess you already know, don't you? I really didn't think you knew." She says quietly, "If you ever want to talk about it, I'm here. Okay?" Then she turns to descend the stairs and make her way to her car.

CHAPTER 17

October 6, 2019

Charleston, SC

VIRGINIA

I tap my long nails on my black phone screen. It's mocking me. I will it to light up with a text, but nothing.

I haven't heard a word from Iris since our girls' night last week.

"I'll text you tomorrow," she had said to me as we hugged goodnight.

And still nothing.

Bennett nudges our big goldendoodle over to make room and curls into our cushy king size bed next to me. Wilks jumps to the floor, irritated, and pads over to his bed in the corner. He can tell by our moods when we're going to let him sleep in the bed with us. Tonight isn't a good night.

I'm laying with my back to him, and I can feel his hesitation to touch me. It's been a little off between us lately. The wedding planning stress is starting to get to him but he won't admit it, and the up and down roller coaster happening between me and Iris has been setting me off.

Why isn't she texting me? I just don't get it. She said she would. I thought things were progressing.

I rack my brain for signs of distaste from her at her house that night, but nothing is coming to mind. It seemed like she had a good time. We talked about so many things, and even talked about college a little.

Well, there's always that, even though I try to forget it.

College.

I start to sweat. Did she not like me when we were at Ole Miss together? Did I do something weird that only she remembers?

I remember seeing her for the first time on Bid Day. A year older than me, she was there with the rest of the girls, welcoming the new class, and she still stood out amongst all the other bright and beautiful faces. Her hair was shorter then and she wore less makeup, but she was one of those effortless girls who looked flawless despite the silly sorority t-shirt she was sporting.

Weeks later, when a rumor spread in my pledge class that I only got a bid to fulfill a minority count, Iris had put them to rest saying *she* was the one who had put a good word in during the selection process.

It may have simmered down the rumors a bit, but I couldn't let go of the nagging sensation inside of me telling me it was true. That I wasn't really good enough to get in.

One drunken night at the house she found me crying in the closet I shared with five other girls and sat in there with me for hours.

"You should have heard some of the things they said about me when I was a freshman," she said as she handed me a scarf from the closet floor to wipe my tears. "Anyone who stands out in any way here is going to have a target on their back. If you were no one to worry about, they wouldn't care enough about you to say anything."

We weren't besties, by any means; she had her own group of sparkly friends. But after that night I felt like we had some kind of understood bond.

Maybe I was wrong. Maybe she didn't like me after all.

My thoughts of the past are interrupted as I feel Bennett inch closer to me until I feel his warm body spooning me. He puts his arm on my hip and kisses my neck sweetly. Even with my cloudy head I still feel the urge to give into him.

We also met at Ole Miss. At a frat party, of course. I was almost through with my sophomore year, and he was a rising senior. He was the tallest and most handsome guy in the room (in the *entire school*, I remember thinking) and I was way too nervous to go and talk to him. I was raised with good self-confidence from my mom who always told me how beautiful I was. "They'll come to you, sweetheart," she would say, but I never really believed it until I saw him look my way from across the room. He did one of those look-away-really-quickly-then-back-a-few-seconds-later looks, and I found myself standing there trying to remember how to breathe.

I close my eyes and let him kiss me as I continue to recall that perfect night.

He was wearing a blue striped button down shirt, khaki shorts and Sperrys, holding a red solo cup of flat Bud Light from a keg. Brown hair cut short. He had asked me my name; that was his opener.

He just said it like that, no hi or anything just, "What's your name?" as if he needed to know right then for a very important reason. As if knowing my name was going to be the answer to something. He wasn't shy or awkward at all, all confidence without even a hint of douche.

I couldn't help myself.

"Virginia." I smiled up at him. I was surprised to see his brown eyes.

"I'm Bennett." He put his cup down on the beer pong table and came a half step closer to me. He towered over my tall-for-a-girl frame, and I wondered how much he could see down my low-cut floral tank top. He continued, "I don't have anything exceptional to say, I'll just warn you. But, I just couldn't stand over there and let the prettiest girl at the party leave without knowing her name."

Stop. He did not just say that. I grabbed at a strand of my long hair and tried to think of a cool response, but he saved me.

"Can I get you another beer?" He smiled a cool, casual smile at me.

"Um, yeah. Let's go."

We found a quieter spot on the porch of the crazy house and talked for an hour while sipping our beers. He was from Charleston, two sisters, had a goldendoodle puppy, and was two years older than me and applying for med school. When he asked about me, he genuinely seemed like he cared. Either that or he was good at faking it. He listened to my struggles with getting enough loans to make college work and my part-time job at the local clothing boutique, my major in English and hopes of being an author, my family and how excited I was to get into this sorority.

"You don't seem like you really belong there. But in a good way," he had said. He meant it as a compliment, but I couldn't help feeling the sting of not fitting in with the girls like I had been striving so hard to do. And the fact that it was obvious to this person who barely knew me. He could tell by the way I stared down at my worn-in sandals from two years ago.

I didn't like that.

He quickly added, "I just mean, you're so smart and driven. My ex is in your sorority, and her only aspiration in life was to earn a solid MRS degree."

Oh, he wasn't talking about appearances. I let out a sigh of relief.

"Oh, that." I chuckled a little. "Well, I don't know about that. You might find me on the street in five years with a sign saying *WILL WRITE FOR FOOD*."

He leaned over and brushed my hair over my tan shoulder and looked at me with the most adorable smile I had ever seen. Our faces were so close I thought he was going to go in for a kiss right then and there, but instead he held my gaze, four brown eyes alone on that porch, the sound of the party fading in the background.

"I think I know exactly where you're going to be in five years, and it's not going to be on the streets."

What a line. But it worked.

Back in our bedroom, Bennett has now become more meaningful with his hands as he grabs for the tie of my silk sleep shorts and brings me back to the present. He yanks at the string and loosens the bow so he can slide them down my thighs. I roll on my back to face him and he pulls himself on top of me, pressing one hand into the pillow to hold himself up while reaching for my silky top with the other. I grab his neck and pull him into me and kiss him firmly.

If I can hold onto the memories of how we were before, of how happy I really was, I can get through this. I don't have to let anything else in the world matter.

Who cares if Iris texts me?

Why can't I get a few minutes without obsessing about her?

I open my eyes and turn my head toward the nightstand and let him kiss my neck. He's distracted; I can reach over and just touch the screen to see if I've missed a text from her, then get back to us.

Can I just wait until after? Can I just enjoy this moment?

My arm half stretched I act like I'm giving in to him. I kiss him again, then turn my neck to his mouth again and reach a little farther. I'm almost there when he stops.

"What are you *doing*?" he asks with an edge to his voice. He presses himself up and looks towards my hand just inches from my phone. I withdraw it quickly. He saw.

"Nothing!" I can't even think of what a normal excuse would be. He knows me too well. He knows what I was doing.

He rolls off of me and sits up, staring at me in disbelief. "This is *insane*, Virginia. You know that, right?" He jumps off of me and out of bed and grabs for his shorts and slams the bathroom door shut behind him.

I'm such an asshole. I sit up and pull my legs into my chest and rest my forehead on my knees. Why do I have to be like this? The wool blanket anxiety is covering me suddenly, and I shakily reach into my bedside table drawer for my little white pills. I swallow three, return the bottle to its home, and pick up my phone.

Still nothing. After a few minutes, I follow him into the bathroom sobbing, real tears, no need to fake it for sympathy points. "I don't know what's wrong with me. It's like…" I can barely get the words out between my sobs. "It's like… I don't know where real life ends and…and…where this other life that I want…begins." He's already holding me against his chest. If I make the first move to apologize, he's always quick to receive it.

"What should I do?" I ask, but I don't really want to know his answer. He doesn't understand this, and he never will. It doesn't matter anyway. I can't give it up. It's mine. But in moments like this, when I know he's going to say I should just give it up, I like to pretend to consider it.

Maybe I will never eclipse Iris or Nella Rose, and sometimes it feels stupid to even be here on this earth trying to be as good as them. I'll never be as rich as Nella Rose or as naturally beautiful as Iris, and it's stupid of me to try so hard to be their friend just to work my way to the top. Why did I even start this whole thing? Why did I have to decide that this is what I wanted to focus all my attention on? I had a fine life before.

"Iris seems like a good person; I know you liked her in college, but remember, I know her too. We were together for years before I knew you. She has nothing that you don't have." He delivers his speech, one that I am expecting. "How can you be so obsessed like this? Constantly checking your phone, it's crazy."

"Bennett, I'm so sorry. I love you. I may not act like it all the time, but you're the most important thing in my life. I promise you're more important to me than her." I try to sound as convincing as possible. “I know my obsession has gotten out of hand. It’s just that, no one prepares you for this job! The girls who make it their entire life are the ones who gain a million followers. They’re the ones who post all the details of their divorces and document every second of their lives. Even though you can tell yourself that it’s sad that they can’t possibly live a genuine life outside of the app, it doesn’t matter because in our world they’re still on top. And, I don’t know, Iris has figured it out and I just keep hoping that by being around here that I will too.”

Bennett tries but he could never really understand, even after all this time watching me.

“So you’re saying, you think that if you make your whole life about your blog, like Iris and Nella Rose, that you’ll be more successful? Would that really be worth it?” he asks.

I pause. It’s something I’ve thought a lot about but it’s hard to explain.

“I don’t know. It feels like it would be.” I look down at my hands.

“I think that’s bullshit.”

CHAPTER 18

March 10, 2020

Mount Pleasant, SC

NELLA ROSE

I'm sitting in my usual spot in my sunroom, convincing myself that I'm working, but really I've been scrolling through Virginia's feed for the past hour.

I study a photo of her and Bennett she posted a few months ago. Of course, you can't trust anything you see on Instagram, but he looks pretty happy in this post. It just blows my mind. Guys like Bennett, from important southern families like the Harolds, marry girls like me or Iris, not Virginia. This is Charleston, not backwoods trash Georgia.

Ever since the remembrance I haven't been able to get her out of my head. I know what she was going to tell me, it couldn't possibly be anything else, and now I hate her even more.

I navigate away from her page and toss my phone next to me on the sofa. I stand, stretch and walk aimlessly down the hall of my house down the hall rug leading past the kitchen, past the sitting room, past the guest bath and into the formal dining room. I stop just inside the doorway.

We have a beautiful dining room. In the center is a huge Victorian mahogany table with matching chairs adorned simply with three antique ginger jars. In one corner of the room sits another heirloom piece my mother gave us as a wedding present, a giant antique china cabinet filled with our wedding china, both sets of our grandparents' wedding china, our formal silver flatware and our Christmas china. By the floor-to-ceiling picture windows sits a grand piano, where Corrinne has her lessons twice a week and Eleanor bangs her chubby hands on the keys the moment I'm trying to have a phone conversation.

The best part of the dining room hangs above the table, our beautiful chandelier. It's from the mid-late 1800s, with cascading bowls of cut crystal and hanging teardrops that sparkle as the morning sun shines, bouncing rainbow specks excitedly all over. They playfully hit Audubon's *White Pelican*, *Black-Backed Gull*, *Fresh-Water Marsh Hen* and *Great White Heron,* my favorite prints from the "Birds of America" series that hang on the back wall. I lift my hand palm up and catch one of the specks of light, holding it there for a minute.

I exhale deeply and turn to leave the room as the doorbell rings.

Weird, I'm not expecting anyone. The girls are at daycare, and Patrick isn't supposed to be back from his business trip for another day. I haven't seen him since his golf tournament. Not that he would ring the doorbell. I straighten myself to see who's there. I'm comfy in my favorite pair of lavender Lululemon leggings and a matching crop top tank. I flex a little as I touch my upper abs peeking through where about an inch of tan midriff is showing.

I don't normally like to answer the door when I'm home alone, but it has been nothing but camera crews since Iris' death, and I've been getting a lot of blog traffic from the media attention. I could use it.

With Iris gone, the golden girl left some sparkly Manolo sandals to fill, and who better to take her place at the top than me?

People in the area know me; I'm also blonde, a mom, a wife, and, if we're being honest, I have the better house. Patrick may not be quite as classically handsome as her hubby John, but he's tall and has that more masculine lumberjack sexiness to him, minus the beard. Iris and I were putting out really similar content, so from now on, people will find what they're looking for from me only.

I feel a faint pang of guilt hit my stomach. She's not just out of the blogging sphere, she's gone. She's gone from this world. It's so much bigger than I'm still able to comprehend even after a few weeks without her.

I pull myself together as I make my way down the foyer to the front door.

Our French doors are glass, but it's that murky privacy glass so I can only see that the figure is a woman. I peek through the peephole and see that it's Detective Holliday. She's looking perfect as usual in a gray fitted knee-length dress with short sleeves. Her hair is pulled back in a smart low ponytail, and she has tiny diamond hoop earrings. She looks like she's about to give the morning weather, not solve a murder. Are detectives supposed to dress so nicely? My only experience is from movies, and they usually dress in ill-fitting, manly pantsuits with bulky shoes.

"Detective," I say, very professionally as I open the door. "What a pleasant surprise. Do you have some news for me?"

"Hi, Nella Rose. May I come in?" Holliday gives me a tight smile with her lips together in only the slightest curve upward.

"Um, yeah, of course. Come on in." I open the pale blue French door for her to step through, "Can I get you some coffee?"

"Coffee would be great, thank you."

We make our way to the kitchen, and I gesture toward the island with my stylish wicker barstools. "Have a seat, please."

She gracefully takes a seat, placing her bag on the counter next to her. Something about her mannerisms make me feel the need to put on my most perfect Southern hostess manners. She can't be more than 40, and yet she has a distinct and evident power in the room between the two of us. My heart is racing a little bit. She makes me nervous.

I turn my back to pour the remainder of the coffee from the pot I made this morning. Just enough for one cup, and it's still fairly warm. I could offer to heat it up in the microwave but that wouldn't be in the best taste. A true Southern hostess would make a new pot and chat pleasantly about the weather while it brews, but I'm too tense for small talk. Before I turn back toward her, I gently push the whiskey bottle behind the coffee pot.

Why is she here? I hope she cuts to the chase; I have my barre class at noon.

"So, to what do I owe the pleasure? Has something new come up in the case?" I hand her the warm mug, a stark white and stylish piece that came with the rest of our casual dish set.

She takes a sip of the coffee and sets it on the marble island. Normally I'd offer a coaster to prevent stains from any spills, but she's so perfectly composed I can't imagine her spilling anything in her life.

"As a matter of fact, yes. We did find something," she says, very evenly. "Your hair was found tangled in Iris' purse chain she had with her when she was found." She stares at me as she delivers her lines. "Well, long blonde hair was found. Seems to be a mix of scalp hair and artificial hair…" She eyes my extra-long strands. Holliday is saying it's partly extension hair, not that she would know a girl like me doesn't use *artificial* extension hair—it's someone's real hair that was sold to the company, dyed and cut to my desired shade and length.

"At first we thought it might be hers, but her DNA doesn't match it. Being that you claim to have been with her in the early evening before her death, we can only assume it's yours," she says, still eyeing my hair up and down from scalp to tip.

I'm blank for a moment. My head tilts a half an inch to the left as I absorb this information. Of course, I could have suspected this.

"Well…I mean, I can see how that happened. We hug a lot. We hugged hello and goodbye twice." I'm still trying to understand why she doesn't see how normal that would be, so I continue. "I have a ton of hair; it gets *everywhere*. Even if it did turn out to be mine, I don't see how it could help the case at all."

She looks down at the mug and touches the handle but doesn't lift it. She's not going to take another sip, I can see that she has more to say.

"It's really not worth discussing too much until we do a DNA match, and I'm sure you don't want to say too much without an attorney present. But, could you just do me the honors, please?" She reaches her hand into her simple black leather tote and retrieves a small plastic baggie. She just holds it for a second—I wonder if she's allowed to do this now without my lawyer—and then extends her arm toward me. I take the bag from her and stand there like an idiot.

I don't know enough about my rights to resist this. I feel like saying no would make me look worse, right? It seems calculated that she came to my house when she probably knew I was home alone, springing something like this on me. Did she do that because she's actually not supposed to ask me for a DNA sample? I wish I'd paid closer attention to those episodes of *Law and Order SVU* I used to binge on in college.

Just agreeing seems to be my best and only option right now. I tuck a piece of hair behind my ear and straighten myself up in a stance of confidence.

"Of course. I have nothing to hide. Like I said, it probably is my hair." I pluck a single strand of my real hair from the scalp and carefully place it in the bag and hand it back to her.

"Thank you, Nella Rose." She stands up and puts the bag safely in her tote. "When the results come back, I'll be in touch for next steps. In the meantime, please stay in Mount Pleasant." We both start to walk back toward the door, as we both can tell that the visit is clearly over.

I'm still so shocked that they are even taking the time to do a DNA test. Does my saying it's probably mine show that I'm not hiding anything? I don't see how it would prove anything or be any use to them.

I open the door and the detective steps out on my grand porch into the sunshine. It's a mild and beautiful spring day, and my flowers are looking beautiful.

"Detective?" I say, getting the courage to ask one more thing. "Can you just tell me why finding one strand of my hair on her purse makes it look like I'm guilty? I'm telling you it was probably mine. You see, I have nothing to hide."

She stands on the porch half turned back to me and pauses for a second before taking her first step down, resting her hand on the railing.

"Because it wasn't just a *strand* of hair found, Nella Rose. It was an unusually large chunk."

CHAPTER 19

October 20, 2019

Mount Pleasant, SC

NELLA ROSE

Across the table, Iris is recalling a hilarious anecdote about her Halloween costume choice. Her green eyes are alive with excitement, her hair, blowing gently in the breeze. We went with a pretty rooftop bar for happy hour tonight, and her flowy baby blue crop top blouse is billowing up, revealing two big freckles on her flat torso. How can she look so graceful while waving her hands around like that? I drop my eyes to my hands. Are they as dainty as hers?

"You should have *seen* the look on this kid's face; his mouth was like WIDE open!" She stops to laugh, and I laugh with her. "That's what I get for wearing a white dress in the sun with a red thong!" She had decided on an angel costume this year and apparently had flashed some teenager on accident.

"Noooo! Oh my gosh, you scarred this kid for life!" I laugh as I slap my hand on my cheek in an exaggerated motion.

"Either that, or ruined him for all other girls!" spits Virginia in her chair next to me.

Wow. So fucking funny, Virginia, I think to myself.

"I think I like that better!" Iris chirped in her sing-song voice she uses when talking to Virginia. For some reason, when *she* is around, Iris becomes like this weird alien version of herself. All pure and sweet. She doesn't do that when it's just us two.

Like last week, after the stupid girls' night incident where they hung out and didn't invite me, Iris fessed up with the truth. I knew she wasn't actually trying to be friends with her.

"Nella Rose, we just ran into each other; it was so not a big deal. Just a last minute whatever thing!" she had said. "She never even answers any of my texts! I don't think she really wants to hang out that much."

Well, she might have me to blame for that one. *Oops.* A month ago on our flight home after New

York, all Iris could talk about was how awesome "Ginny" was and how we should hang out with her more, how when she knew her in college, she could just tell she was a diamond in the rough and would be a great project for her. How she was jealous of her naturally long and thick hair. How sweet she and Bennett were. How cute her gray coat was and how she was going to get one like it. How her pictures were so unique. And so on and so on AND SO ON.

Like, HELLO Iris, I'm right here! Would you really rather hang out with her than me? I had thought on the plane as I listened to her blabber on inserting my "mmhms" every now and then to make me not seem like a bitch.

I couldn't take it anymore, and while she was in the bathroom, I grabbed her phone from the seat back pocket, typed in her code and went to Virginia's contact. Just a simple tap and she was blocked. She would never get a text that Iris would send, and Iris would never get a call or text from her.

Iris is so ditzy; she'll never think to check into that. She'll just think Virginia is ignoring her texts and their "friendship" will fade away like it never happened. It's definitely one of the crazier things I've ever done, but come on! We don't need her; she totally brings down our stock.

"What are you dressing up as, Nella Rose?" At the sound of Iris' canary voice I'm brought back to our table at happy hour.

"I'm going to be a snow queen!" I say. "I have an awesome girl doing my makeup."

"Ah, that's awesome! We'll both be in white! That'll be so cute for pictures!" Iris squeals.

I know it will, which is obviously why I chose it. We'll just have to get photos together.

Virginia smiles in agreement, looking a little awkward. She's waiting for us to ask her what she's going to be, but I obviously don't care, and neither does Iris.

"I was thinking of being Audrey Hepburn from *My Fair Lady*," she states, without anyone asking her. "The dress from the end when she goes to the fancy party."

"AH! You're going to be so gorgeous! Isn't that dress also white?" Iris shrieks in excitement. I roll my eyes in frustration. I don't know if it's white; I've never seen that movie. Obsessions with Audrey Hepburn are so high school.

"It's like gold with a lot of silver accents. I found it on Etsy! It's really a beautiful dress; I'm so excited about it." She takes out her phone and scrolls through her photos to show Iris.

"WOW! That is so stunning, Ginny!" Iris beams as she leans over the table to look at the photos.

I clench my fists under the table.

After the fifth time in a row carefully dodging her requests to include Virginia on our dinners and happy hours, I figured I had to ask her myself or Iris would figure out that something weird was going on. I just have to breathe and smile and laugh and get through this one night, and hopefully I won't have to see her again for another month or so. Or ever.

❀

Charleston, SC

VIRGINIA

That was a strange two hours, I think as I hook Wilks' leash to his collar to take him on an evening walk. I've just gotten home from our "happy" hour, although someone at our table didn't make it seem very happy. Nella Rose is so possessive over Iris. Every time I opened my mouth she would check her phone or interrupt me or roll her eyes when she thought I wasn't looking.

Obviously, if I want Iris to let me in, Nella Rose is going to have to be on board too.

Why is there always something in my way?

The sun is going to set in about two hours, which is just enough time to pop over to Mount Pleasant and get Wilks some exercise.

It's a pretty evening, I think as I load him up in my SUV. His fluffy golden locks are freshly groomed, and he happily takes his place in the backseat, panting with excitement. It's just beginning to feel like fall in the South, and by that, I mean the temperature has dropped in the 60s to 70s.

I decide on a light blue long sleeve athletic shirt and short white shorts and throw my hair up in a messy-cute ponytail.

I use these walks as my time to myself, time to think or plan or get inspiration. Especially lately. Things have been moving so fast with the wedding and everything. Our date is June 27, 2020, and planning is in crunch time right now, but I find myself spending more time on other things.

I think back to that night a few weeks ago when Bennett caught me checking my phone in bed as I scoot in the driver seat and put the car in drive. I've been putting my role of the doting fiancé into overdrive to smooth things over between us, starting with upping the amount of sex we're having. Sometimes twice a day, which, for a doctor with a crazy schedule and a lunatic with a prescription addiction, is pretty great.

I've been working on it, but if he knows me at all, I'm sure he's noticed the strain.

I'll bet it wasn't like this with Iris.

Ugh, Iris. He has her to compare me to.

The fact that they dated before us was something Bennett and I never talked about, and it *certainly* wasn't mentioned by me or Iris. They were together for two years, and the only thing I really knew about the relationship was why they broke up.

He had dumped her for cheating. "That's right," he had said. "She accidentally sent me a topless photo of herself with the text, *Bennett just left, come over*. As far as I'm concerned, she's nothing." That's all he's ever said about them together.

I'd tried my best to dig up whatever I could about them back in college, but social media was barely a thing then. There were maybe a few old photos of them, but that was it, nothing that could really tell me anything about them. I'd given up and had no plans to pry anymore with Bennett.

After sitting at a brief stoplight, I turn right into Iris and Nella Roses' neighborhood. I whiz past Iris' house (it's more at the start of the neighborhood, so there's no avoiding it) and drive down the beautiful lanes of Plantation Meadows before pulling into my normal parking spot in a vacant cul-de-sac where new houses are being built. Nella Rose lives safely a few streets away so I can easily navigate around the bigger, older waterfront houses. There would be no reason for her to drive this way unless she was going to Iris', and Iris said she was putting Ivory to bed and going to sleep early after our happy hour.

"Ready to go, Wilks?!" He is pacing in the backseat like a madman. I take one glance at my phone to check if NR has revealed her whereabouts anytime recently, plug my headphones in and tuck it in the pocket of my shorts. I decide some indie rock jams would be good music for this pretty evening. I hit shuffle.

As we walk past gorgeous mansion after gorgeous mansion, the same houses we see three times a week on our walks, I start to wonder about the owners inside.

Like I always do.

The ideal couples and families, like Iris and John or Nella Rose and Patrick. I stick my hand out a little and look down at my engagement ring. It sits on my tan hand gleaming in the evening light of the golden hour as Wilks pulls me along the sidewalk excitedly. It's the kind of diamond that belongs in this neighborhood, I decide. Big and classic.

Looking to my left, I see a young woman in a little tennis outfit retrieve the mail. She waves at me, friendly. She's beautiful. I'd love to look like her when I'm older.

I wave back.

Next door, I see two middle-aged men arranging furniture on their deck. They're laughing at a joke I'll never know. I continue on unnoticed by them.

I have to look more carefully for the couple at the next house, but I find them perched together in rocking chairs on the second story porch. They're younger, in their thirties, and the brown-haired husband is staring at his phone while his pretty wife talks at him.

Wilks tugs at his leash as we turn a corner. The jingle of his collar radiates throughout the quietness of the street. Without our disturbance, only the rustling of the trees in the fall breeze would be heard. As we continue down the street we pass a grand brick house. The construction is almost complete; someone will be moving here in a few months if I had to guess.

I stop to face the house and close my eyes. I picture the 30-something son of a politician. His name is Daniel. He has dark brown eyes and short black hair swooped to the side with a touch of hair gel. On his arm is a 20-something Southern belle named Lisa. Her father gave them the money for the down payment, even though she didn't need the help. She's an accomplished writer with 16 published cookbooks. They'll have the perfect life together here.

I'm so enraptured in my fantasy that I've forgotten my normal path, and I realize I'm standing a house away from Nella Rose's. *Shit.* Turning on my heels I tug at Wilks' neck to pull him back in the direction we came. Unless she and Iris made plans secretly without me after happy hour, she's probably home right now. I'm so close to the end of the street, I just have to make it there, and I can disappear from the view of her house. Sweat starts to bead across my forehead.

"Virginia?"

I snap my neck toward the sound of my name and see to my dismay the one person I was hoping to avoid. *Shit shit shit shit.*

"Hey, Nella Rose!" I try to sound as casual as possible, but this is so freaking awkward. I have no explanation for being here.

She jogs toward me in a tiny workout set. Around her little waist is a running band, holding her phone, and she takes out one AirPod as she approaches. She's obviously been on a jog around the neighborhood, something I didn't realize she did. Her long blonde locks have been carefully woven into dutch braid pigtails that hang down her delicate back that doesn't seem to have a trace of sweat.

"Were you coming over to see me?" she asks in an exasperated tone. One hand on her hip, she looks down at her watch to check her heart rate, I'm guessing, then looks back up at me.

"Oh, heh…no." I allow an awkward giggle. "Is this your street?"

"Um, yeah. That's my house." She points a manicured finger in the direction of her gates. Cocking her head a little she gives me a little raise of her thick eyebrows and a thin-lipped smile. I can almost hear her saying *poor thing, you've been caught.*

"Oh wow, how funny! No, um, I was just taking Wilks for a playdate with my friend, but she had to cancel at the last minute. I decided to walk him a little instead, since it's so nice out," I say, and it sounds pretty convincing. I'm impressed with myself for my quick thinking.

She narrows her eyes a little, not seeming too convinced.

"Right," she says.

"Yeah, funny bumping into you. Tonight was fun!" It's the thing you always say to girls after a happy hour or something, reassuring the fact that you had fun and promising the hope of a next time.

"Uh-huh. Well, I'd better get home. I don't wanna leave Patrick with the girls for too long," she says, and without a goodbye, she tucks her AirPod back in her ear and jogs off down the sidewalk toward her house.

I feel humiliated. She must think I'm some stalker now. I need to be more careful about my route next time.

CHAPTER 20

March 10, 2020

Mount Pleasant, SC

NELLA ROSE

I'm dumbfounded as I sit alone on the steps of my porch. Detective Holliday is long gone, and the sun is high in the sky. I've missed my barre class for sure, but that's not what's concerning me.

An unusually large chunk. That's what she had called it. They found *an unusually large chunk* of *my* hair tangled in the chain of Iris' purse when she was found strangled in the front yard of her house, which is only a few streets away from mine.

I keep recounting the information that I have over and over: They found Iris in front of her house, strangled, early in the morning, with my hair in her purse chain, and I have no alibi because our security cameras were broken. I guess Iris and John are not as paranoid as Patrick and me because they didn't have any cameras of their own, and with the houses so spread apart, her neighbors didn't catch anything of note, yet.

I realize I'm clutching the banister of the staircase so hard my hand is starting to hurt.

I have nothing to worry about. We have a great lawyer, having so much to protect. I'll call her when I get my thoughts together, but my mind won't stop going back to that night in November. That incident, which could still come out, doesn't exactly paint me in the best light.

Fucking Virginia. I can see her deciding to come forward about that even though it's been months. I slam my fist into my forehead, trying to force the memory of that night out of my head.

It's her fault! If she would have just stopped being so fucking annoying, everything would have been fine and I'd only have my alibi to worry about.

CHAPTER 21

November 12, 2019

Charleston, SC

VIRGINIA

I watch Bennett in the dim candlelight cutting a thick bite from his filet and dip it in buttery sauce before taking a bite. He's wearing his nice dinner jacket over a crisp white shirt, and I'm falling for him all over again.

Things have been really good lately. Not just with Bennett. Things are starting to change.

Things have been great with Iris, surprisingly.

One night about two weeks ago she randomly texted me out of the blue with shrieking all caps, *GINNY! YOU WERE BLOCKED ON MY PHONE!?*

What? What does that even mean? I wondered as I stared at the text bubble in disbelief. I had begun to accept that she just didn't like me after watching her and Nella Rose hang out over and over again without inviting me. The happy hour was all I had gotten, and I started to wonder if Nella Rose told Iris how she saw me walking in Plantation Meadows outside her house. Almost every day I saw their perfect smiling faces on my feed, and slowly the acceptance had begun to dull the ache inside.

But that text sent me swirling back into her world.

We texted for like an hour, and she explained how one day she was so annoyed with me for never answering her texts that she decided to see if she had my number right in her phone and saw that I was blocked!

"So I never got anything from you, and you never got anything from me! I don't know what could have happened!"

Really? I had thought. I had a pretty good guess. *Your* friend. That double-named bitch Nella Rose did it. I was sure of it.

Of course, I never said that and just relished in our first text conversation in a long time that ended in her inviting me over to hang out. We hung out every few days for weeks. We went on bike rides, she came over for wine nights, we took photos for each other, we grabbed cupcakes together, and she and Nella Rose hadn't seen much of each other at all. Also, I kept gaining more followers every time she posted me.

Everything is falling back into place. Things are good with both her and Bennett.

I'm so close to getting everything I want. I can almost taste it.

Bennett had decided randomly that we should go out to eat at our favorite steak house to celebrate the six-month anniversary of our engagement. I picked out a low-cut black dress that hugged my hips and fell right above my knees. The back was exposed, and the straps came together in a halter style behind my neck. We walked out to his truck together hand in hand.

And here we are, sharing a $150 bottle of wine and chatting happily between bites of our $55 steaks. Surrounding us at identical tables are bustling groups of businessmen, cute young couples on first dates and chic older couples who probably come here once a week.

He puts his fork down and grabs his glass of wine as he looks at me.

"Let's toast," he begins, and I lift my glass as well. "To the best six months of my life."

"Cheers." I smile, and we clink our glasses together and take a sip.

I feel my phone buzzing in my black sequinned clutch. I'll check it later.

"So," he says after a sip of wine. "I have a question for you."

I set down my glass carefully on the white tablecloth and look at him in the dim candlelight. "Oh yeah, what's that?" I take a generous helping of Brussel sprouts and spoon them onto my plate with a clink.

"Why didn't you tell me that you saw Nella Rose last month?" he says, not looking at me.

"Um, I'm not sure what you mean. I went to that happy hour with her and Iris, you know that." The pressure of my heart in my chest is overwhelming. Why would he know I saw her outside her house?

"I ran into Patrick at the driving range. He said that you and Nella Rose bumped into each other on the street outside their house. You were walking Wilks?" He's still not looking at me, trying to ease me into this. He's caught me in a lie.

The truth is, I had told him I was taking Wilks to a dog park in James Island, which is the opposite direction of Plantation Meadows.

"Oh, right." I try to think of the best way to phrase this so that I don't sound too insane. "I just changed my mind about the dog park. I thought it would be fun to walk him in Plantation Meadows, maybe scout out some houses."

His eyes light up at this. "Really? I thought you said you definitely didn't want to live there. What brought this on?"

I know he's always wanted us to live there.

"I don't know, I guess you just got to me with the whole school thing. If we want our kids to have the best education someday, that is the better place to be.

You were right. But I'm not promising anything! I was just looking." Lie, lie, lie. But it's enough to get him off my back for now.

CHAPTER 22

November 12, 2019

Charleston, SC

NELLA ROSE

She's making me want to barf more than usual as I see her brown hair pop up on my feed. Who goes to a place like Hammond's just for a six-month anniversary of getting engaged?! It's so pathetic. Patrick and I used to go there every week before the girls were born. It's not *that* fancy, but to them it's a special occasion place. I mulled these thoughts over three whiskey sours I had earlier.

I haven't been able to get her out of my head. I guess Iris found out she was blocked on her phone because they have been spending, like, every waking moment together for the past few weeks. I try to stay calm as I quickly walk down the isle of the supermarket. I've never been to this one before, so I'm having trouble finding them.

My mind darts back and forth between a million thoughts. How did she find out about Virginia being blocked? Did she think that I did it? Is that why she hasn't asked me to hang out? Is that why she has been ignoring my texts? Did Virginia talk some shit about me and make her think less of me?

I frantically grab for my phone in my Chanel. My hands are shaking, and I'm having trouble finding it. The warm rush of the whiskey has transformed my body into slow molasses, and my hands aren't keeping up with my thoughts. I finally find it and stop for a second to scroll through my page. Just to check for any more updates.

I realize I'm sweating as I quickly pace down the aisles. I tuck a lock of my greasy bangs behind my ear as my eyes dart back and forth around the store. I never showered after my run today, and I am gross right now. Where *are* they??

I see them and practically run across the store. I grab every single one that they have. Some look better than others, but it doesn't matter, they'll do just fine. I take them to the cashier and hand over a shiny credit card, wobbling a little side to side as I wait for her to finish ringing them up.

As I exit the store into the late evening light, I catch a glimpse of myself in a car door mirror. I'm a wreck. My outfit is a disaster. I have no makeup on and dark purple circles sit angrily under my eyes. I have my long hair in a cute-messy pony, minus the cute. I really hope no one recognized me here.

My mind has been on things other than my appearance right now. Like, *oh, I don't know*, the bitch who is stealing my best friend!?

I climb into my Range Rover, place my purchases in the front seat next to me, and pull out my phone again. I go to the maps and my home address is suggested for me, but I don't choose it. I put in a different address and start up the car.

❀

VIRGINIA

Bennett and I are talking about the hotel blocks for the wedding as we make our way to the front door of our house. He's holding my hand, and I'm craning my neck up to him. "I love that place by the Harbor!

Do you think our families would pay that much per night?"

Suddenly I feel the jerk of his hand as he stops us in our tracks. I almost fall backward in my stilettos but he holds me up firmly.

"Wha…" I'm about to ask him what's wrong when I peel my eyes away from his face and look at our front doorstep.

What the fuck. I don't get it.

Irises are everywhere. There have to be a hundred of them. Purple, but not pretty.

They're cut up, destroyed, stomped on, ripped apart and sprawling all over our doorstep, spilling into the sidewalk.

I start to slowly step forward but Bennett stops me again. "What the fuck is this?" He's looking around. It hasn't occurred to me that someone could still be here. Who would do this?

The image of a tiny frame scattering the flowers, tearing them to shreds with a hateful smile on her face suddenly takes over my thoughts. I think I know exactly who did this.

"Nella Rose." I say it out loud because I don't think Bennett has caught up.

Nella Rose always seemed like she had this anger hidden beneath her calm and cool surface, and most of the time, it was directed at me. For what, I wasn't sure before, but staring at the floral massacre before me I suddenly understood completely. It was always about Iris. Me coming between her and Iris.

Bennett is grabbing for his phone to dial the police, and I'm going to let him. This is fucking psychotic. Let the police come and tarnish her perfect reputation with a harassment charge. Maybe then Iris would kick her to the curb for good, and there would be room for a new Flower Girl in Iris' life. Permanently. With no distractions.

But I decide to stop him. Is this really a crime? It's definitely weird and creepy, but not threatening.

Grabbing his arm, I say, "B, it's not like she vandalized our house. It's just flowers. What would we say to the police?"

He looks back at me. "Baby, this is the work of a crazy person. She might come back and do something worse."

"I don't think she's capable of actually *hurting* anyone. She's just jealous of me and Iris' friendship," I say.

"Just jealous? This is like crazy-ex-girlfriend-who-comes-and-kills-you-in-your-sleep shit." He raises his voice, and I hush him so he doesn't wake up our neighbors.

"Shh, I know it's crazy, but I'm not scared of her. I really don't think we have anything to worry about. If anything else happens then we'll report it. Okay?" I say steadily. I realize I don't want any bad blood here. Iris might take her side and say I made the whole thing up.

I can tell he's not convinced, but he locks his phone in a silent agreement and puts his arm on my lower back to lead me inside. I take a few steps forward, kicking up purple petals, but the feeling of something poking my big toe through my strappy heels surprises me, and I stop us both. It's not the feeling of the soft flowers. It's harder and has a pointy edge. I look down. Peeking up through the slain irises is a speck of white.

"What's that?" Bennett asks, wondering why I've stopped cold in my tracks.

I hesitate for a second but gain the courage to bend down and pick up the piece of paper. I should have known. People like Nella Rose don't just leave a display like this anonymously. She wants to make sure I know It's her, without any real proof, of course. Something only I'll understand. Something you can't explain to anyone else.

The paper is folded in half, like the notes you hand your friends in middle school, and Bennett silently watches me as I open.

In blue pen, written in tiny all-caps letters, read just four words:

BACK OFF, STALKER BITCH.

I thought Bennett was the only one who knew about that, but I guess I was wrong. Iris must have told Nella Rose. No wonder. She thinks *I'm* the crazy one.

I think back to college.

The night after Iris comforted me in that closet was one of the best nights of my life at that point. Learning how she was the one who vouched for me and helped me get into our sorority, how nice she was despite her insanely gorgeous looks, all her perfect clothes, her perfect hair, all her friends, it was all too much. I wanted to be like her.

It started innocently enough. I would lie in bed in the sorority house on my laptop scouring the internet for traces of her. Where she went to high school. What sports she played (cheerleading and volleyball). Her Family. Her childhood dog. Her favorite food. I copied her clothes. Everything. I even thought about bleaching my brown hair, but I found out it would have cost like $300, which I couldn't afford. I just wanted to be like this girl that everyone liked. What I was doing clearly wasn't working, so what was wrong with finding some inspiration?

That's all that Bennett knows—that I was a little obsessed with Iris, which is why I was always comparing myself, and why it hurt so much that she had found a new friend. That she had found someone better.

But, as it goes, things got a little worse.

There was something about being with a guy she had been with that kept occupying my thoughts, a guy who had been good enough for her to date for two whole years. A guy like that, I thought, is my ticket. Of course, she never told me that she cheated on him.

I learned his name, his frat, his favorite coffee shop, and eventually I caught his attention at a party, one I knew he'd be at. I had worn my skimpiest outfit (boys are boys) and flirted my heart out while still trying to be cool. I talked up my smarts and innocence in the hopes that he would find me bright and sparkly compared to Iris' only two known flaws. Her infidelity and low IQ.

Bennett.

Falling in love with him was never part of the plan. I never thought that far ahead.

CHAPTER 23

March 11, 2020

Mount Pleasant, SC

NELLA ROSE

The sound of the phone startles me, and I make my way to the kitchen from my spot next to Patrick in the sitting room. We are watching a movie with the girls. Well, the girls and I are watching as Patrick scrolls through his phone, looking at sports videos.

"Nella Rose?"

"Yes, speaking." I try to sound cool. I'm pretty good at faking it by now.

"This is Detective Holliday." As if I didn't already know that.

"Good evening, Detective. It's a little late. What can I do for you?" I'm irritated. I look back to the sitting room at Eleanor squirming on Patrick's lap, laughing noisily, and Corrinne leaning her head on his shoulder. Patrick has been less than concerned with the fact that Holliday paid me a visit, and doesn't even look up when he hears me on the phone with her.

"I'm very sorry to call at this time, I just wanted to confirm the existence of your DNA found on the deceased Iris Sutten." So formal. She must be around a colleague she's trying to impress. Or maybe this is just her all the time. "The hair on her purse chain matches that of the sample you provided. The hair is now considered our prime source of evidence in the case."

I hadn't considered that this was the only bit of evidence they had found. They had spent two fucking days with Iris' front yard sanctioned off, looking for fingerprints, footprints, blood, tire tracks. After all of that, nothing came up that would lead them to any suspects? I find it hard to believe, but I guess it must be true.

"I'm calling as a courtesy, because I know you have small children you might need to make arrangements for…" Is she waiting for me to put the dots together? "But tomorrow we will be coming by to escort you to the station for questioning."

I sit and let her listen to my silence on the other end of the line. How is this possibly happening to me?

Finally, I say, “Y’all are insane. But, it seems I don’t have a choice.”

❀

The fluorescent lights can’t be doing good things for my skin tone. I touch my finger gently to the frown lines I’ve developed between my eyebrows over the past few years. I’ve been holding off on Botox, but I’m thinking it’s time to start. I’ll make an appointment with my dermatologist next week.

My hand retreats to my lap , folds in with its partner, and I squeeze them tightly together nervously. My sky blue Prada bag is perched on the table beside me while I sit in an uncomfortable plastic chair, the kind you find attached to a desk in grade school, in a room alone with an obvious two-way mirror.

It seems like hours before Detective Holliday finally enters the room. She’s followed by some chubby police officer whose pants are doing some serious work against his large middle section and a tall and powerful-looking blonde woman with a briefcase. As usual, Holliday looks incredible. She's wearing a perfectly-tailored plum jacket over a white blouse and matching plum skirt, no panty hose, and a pair of black patent leather Christian Louboutins.

I'm glad I dressed up. I decided on a blush pleated midi skirt and a lace camisole. Nude, soft leather peep-toe platform sandals give me an extra few inches. I wore my good diamond earrings, the ones I brought to New York. I reach up to touch one with my pointer finger, the cool feeling of the large stone puts me at ease.

"Mrs. Miller, this is Detective Marshall and Officer Henley. They're here to accompany me for your interview."

"Hello, it's nice to meet you both," I say as I stand to shake their hands. "Under the circumstances, I guess."

Holliday breezes over my comment. "Why don't we get started. I'm sure you'd like to make it home before supper."

"Whatever you say." I smile.

They all sit down, with both pretty female detectives taking a place at the table across from me, and the officer takes a seat in the corner. It's Holliday who begins.

"So, we discussed a few things in your interview at your house last week. But, I'd like to dive into more detail about exact times, exact places, you know, that sort of thing. Does that sound good?"

"Sure." Stay cool.

"Okay, so we have you going to happy hour with Iris around 3:00 p.m. on February 25, 2020 at a place called The Watch. Can you tell me what time you left?"

"Yes, it was 5:30 p.m.. I remember because rush hour traffic on the bridge was a nightmare, so I checked the time to make sure I didn't do this again. It was awful. I sat there for almost an hour."

"Okay, that's helpful. And where were you going?" Detective Jehli speaks up now.

"I was going home. Patrick, my husband, gets home from work around 6:30 p.m., and I needed to start cooking. I remember this vividly. The traffic made me late, so Patrick was home with the girls by the time I arrived."

"And you went straight home from The Watch? No stops along the way?"

Shit, I did make one stop, I forgot about that. Should I even mention it? The hesitation seems worse, so I answer honestly, "Oh, yes, I did stop at…at the liquor store." I stumble over my words a little in embarrassment. Stopping by to get booze on my way home from a bar wasn't very becoming of a mother.

This doesn't seem to faze Holliday, but Detective Marshall perks up. The officer sits silently in the corner looking bored.

"Okay. And exactly which liquor store was that? You know, you failed to mention that in your interview." Marshall is now studying me.

"Yes, I had forgotten about it. It just occurred to me now." It was still hours before the murder happened. I left it out because it didn't seem relevant. "It was the one over on Coleman Boulevard. By the entrance of Plantation Meadows."

"Did anything *else* happen that evening that didn't occur to you until today?" Marshall has taken over the interview. Her long blonde hair is up neatly in a ponytail, and her brown eyes are all business. She has one of those faces that pulls off a ponytail. I don't find myself wishing she would take it down like I normally would when a woman has such nice hair.

"No, nothing out of the ordinary happened," I say.

There's a pause. Marshall looks over at Holliday, who takes over from there.

"The thing is, we are really confused as to how so much of your hair could have gotten stuck in her purse, when you claim it's probably just from a hug goodbye." Marshall opens her briefcase and pulls out a piece of paper with codes and writing on it too small for me to read across the table. "You see how that doesn't make much sense?"

Holliday continues, "We are also interested in knowing why your security footage was turned off earlier that evening. You see, this document indicates the activity on your account that day, and here," she points at a paragraph toward the end of the page, "shows that a user on the account, from your home IP address, deactivated them on the evening of February 25, 2020."

What? This is the first I'm hearing of this, and I'm sure my face is showing it.

"Um, I'm sorry, I'm confused. Patrick, he…he said that the cameras had broken." I feel a tinge of sweat start to form between my shoulder blades.

"No, I'm afraid not." Holliday still has her hand on the corner of the paper, and she slides it towards me to take a look. I keep my eyes up.

"The cameras have been turned off several evenings by a user on the account over the past eight months, only to be turned back on the next morning. Every morning, except the morning of Iris's death. The cameras have not been turned back on since then, but there is a log of a call to the security company…" Marshall pulls out another sheet of paper, a call log, "the morning that Iris was found."

I sit there dumbfounded. I've never turned off the cameras, not that I would even know how. Patrick set us both up with an account so we could log in and make changes, but I never concerned myself with it. Why would he be turning it on and off randomly and so often, and more importantly, why was it conveniently turned off that night and never turned back on?

Marshall studies my face and continues, "You can see how this is adding up from our perspective, yes?"

I sit there, squeezing my diamond earring between my thumb and pointer finger. None of this is making any sense to me, but I try to remain calm. Yes, okay, I do know why there could be a chunk of my hair stuck on her purse, but it's not related to the cameras. I have no idea how to answer, but I do know what I need to say next. I reach for my Prada and stand up out of my child's chair.

"I think I need to call my lawyer."

CHAPTER 24

November 13, 2019

Charleston, SC

VIRGINIA

Bennett left for the hospital early, and I decided to spend the day at home. He felt a little uneasy leaving me there after the psycho display with the irises that Nella Rose left for me last night, but I assured him I would be fine.

I sit at my computer in a cushioned barstool at our kitchen island, willing the words to come, but I'm way too distracted. I save my book draft and close it so I can open a new tab.

Iris is on a trip to Savannah with her sister, according to her feed. She just posted the cutest photo of them together by River Street. She's wearing the prettiest sage green coat over dark denim cuffed jeans and simple brown booties. Her caption reads, *there's nothing like family time.*

Hasn't she worn that green coat before? I think it might be from last year.

I mouse over and pull up Nella Rose's page. She just posted a photo of her and her daughters standing in front of one of those cute painted houses in downtown Charleston.

I stayed up all night trying to figure out what exactly Nella Rose knows. The words *Stalker Bitch* keep replaying over and over in my head. Bennett had asked what it meant, but I breezed over it, saying she just must be nuts.

"Who knows, you have to be crazy to pull a stunt like this."

But I had told Iris a long time ago about my tiny obsession with her (minus the Bennett part, of course), and I think she had actually found it cute. She told me she wouldn't tell a soul, but she must have told Nella Rose. Figures.

And now that Iris and I have become friends, Nella Rose has gotten so jealous that she's trying to split up our friendship by bringing up my embarrassing past? I may be a lot of things but *stalker* is not one of them.

I snap my laptop closed and press my fingers to my temples.

Should I call her? Or maybe go over there? How do you handle something as weird as this? If Nella Rose had any sense, she would deny the whole thing. I took a photo of the flowers last night, but that doesn't really prove anything.

At this point, I guess there's just nothing to be done.

❀

Mount Pleasant, SC

NELLA ROSE

I squint and will the rising sun to go back down. The light is like hellfire, reminding me that I haven't been hungover like this in forever.

My late-night visit to Virginia's house is a blurry memory that I'm trying to convince myself was just a bad dream. Sometimes you just snap, right? Something about seeing them together had sent me spiraling downward. I was falling, and I had to do something to gain control again and it was all I could come up with.

I roll onto my stomach and pull the silk pillowcase over my head to get some relief from the light when I realize it was the sun that had woken me up, which means the alarm clock didn't go off.

I sit up too fast, that jolt you get when you're late in the morning, and look around the room. The clock on the wall taunts 7:25 a.m., and Patrick's spot next to me in the bed is empty and cold. He's gotten up before me, which is never a good sign.

I hurl myself out of bed and grab my blue robe from the back of the door, throwing it open to find Patrick standing in the hallway, staring at me. He's holding a mug of coffee and casually leaning against the banister.

"Good morning, wife." He looks me up and down with a sneer. "Nice of you to wake up, finally."

"The girls, have th…"

He interrupts me, "Amber came by 20 minutes ago to get the girls for daycare." His face is cold. "Here's your coffee. I took the liberty of adding a little hair of the dog for you." He starts to walk toward me slowly with the mug extended. I don't know how to talk my way out of this one.

Just before he reaches me, he throws the mug hard into the wall next to me. Hot coffee sprays everywhere, burning my arm, and I recoil, holding up the robe to cover my face from the shattering glass. It all happens in an instant, and before I've realized what's going on, Patrick has one arm on my shoulder and pins me against the wall with a thud.

"*Why* do you keep making me do this to you?" His face is inches from mine as he yells. My eyes are squeezed shut—I can't bear to look at him like this—and in another instant, he's throwing me down to the ground. I land on my left hip, and my head hits the wood floor, hard.

"If you're so tired, why don't you lay down right there and take a nap."

I do as he says; there's no use getting up right now, he'll just throw me back down.

He squats down next to me, and I stay frozen. I need to play dead, I tell myself. I keep my eyes closed and try not to cry yet.

"I want a wife, Nella Rose. Someone to take care of our children. Someone to keep up the house. You're just not holding up your end. You realize that, right? What do you expect when you act like this? I won't let our girls have a mother who comes home blackout drunk and sleeps in till noon. Where the hell were you last night?"

He's right about that. Sometimes that nightcap turns into two, and I'm left alone with my thoughts, which is a dangerous place for me to be. I did all of this—the marriage, the blog, the children—because I thought it would make me happy, but I started seeing that I might be the unhappiest person in the world. The thought of losing my one friend, the girl who keeps me sane and lets me vent to her about everything, just set me off.

So, I make another and another, until all my whiskey is gone and I have to go buy more, and I find myself where I did last night. I didn't mean to get so caught up in Virginia and Iris, and my floral display on her porch…that obviously wasn't my greatest moment.

I might hate Virginia, but that was a lot. Yeah, Iris told me about how Virginia was obsessed with her in college, and I always held onto that little bit of information because it was a secret between us, but now I look like the crazy one. If Virginia tells Iris about the flowers, I might as well kiss our friendship goodbye for good.

I try to stay focused on Iris and Virginia, distracting myself from my current scene.

Patrick is still squatting by my sprawled-out body on the floor. My arms are over my face, hiding from the humiliation and the potential of more blows, but suddenly I feel him touch my shoulder softly.

I open my eyes to see his face close to mine.

"Tell me where you were," he says.

"I-I just went to Virginia's house. Just to hang out a bit." He knows nothing about my friends.

He glares at me for a moment before straightening himself back up, leaving me on the ground.

"Well, the next time you get shit-faced like that, you'd better be able to wake your ass up the next morning."

❀

I don't know how long I lay there after Patrick leaves. An hour? Three? But I finally find the strength to rise off the hard floor. My shoulder aches from hitting the wall, and I rub the side of my head to see if there's any blood. It just seems to be bruised.

In the bathroom, I take in the damage.

My eyes are red and swollen from crying the past few hours, but that's not the worst part of my appearance. I just reek of a hungover aging woman. Twenty-eight might be young, but the morning after a binge like that leaves me looking haggard. I don't bounce back like I used to. My lips are dry and cracked. There's a bruise already forming at my hairline on my left temple.

I lean over the sink and start to cry again, but I'm reminded that I have a lot to do before everyone gets home tonight, and I stop myself.

The girls will not come home to a deadbeat mother again, Patrick is right. And I need to call Virginia and smooth things out. What if she decided to call the cops, or worse, tell Iris? I splash some water on my face, apply moisturizer and lip balm, and head to the bedroom to retrieve my phone.

"Hello?" Virginia answers. She knows it's me, but she's acting coy with her casual greeting. I'll bet she's really interested to hear what I have to say.

"Hey." I don't really know how to start a conversation like this. "Look, I know you probably guessed it was me who left that…um, those…flowers on your doorstep?"

"Um, yeah. I had an instinct." She stops, waiting for me to continue.

"Look, I'm really embarrassed. It's just…" What is it? "I'm just, having a hard time…er, it's just hard for me to feel like I'm losing Iris. I know that doesn't make any sense to you probably, and it definitely doesn't excuse my behavior…"

"No, it definitely doesn't. That was some crazy shit, Nella Rose."

Ugh, I knew this girl was a bitch. She's not even going to let me apologize, I think, until she continues after a big sigh.

"But, I sorta get it. I feel a little crazy when I see you and Iris hanging out without me. And when I put it together with how you blocked me on her phone…"

I cut her off, I'm not gonna fess up to that. "What? What are you talking about? I didn't block you," I lie.

"Oh…" She sounds like she might believe me. "Iris had just told me I had been randomly blocked on her phone, which is why we weren't getting each other's calls or texts. I assumed you had done that."

"Girl, no way. I didn't do anything that crazy. She's such a spaz, I'm sure she did it herself by accident." That line came out way too easily.

"You're right," she's chuckling. She totally believes me. "That does sound like something she would do."

"Totally! That's so weird; she never mentioned that happened." We both laugh a little. This has gone perfectly. "Anyway, I just feel really weird about what I did. Can we forget the whole thing ever happened?"

She pauses, but finally answers, "Sure. Water under the bridge."

I sigh in relief. But, I have to add one last thing. I have to make sure I don't lose her, even if that means I have to share her with Virginia.

"Um, also…is there any way we can leave Iris out of this?"

She pauses before answering, but finally says, "Yeah, there's no reason she should know."

CHAPTER 25

March 11, 2020

Mount Pleasant, SC

NELLA ROSE

I set my phone down on the side table next to my perch in the sunroom. I've just had a long call with our lawyer, and she explained to me the next steps. They're basically going to wait another few days to try and collect evidence, and if anything else comes up that makes me look guilty, they'll make the arrest.

I sit and stare at a painting on the wall. It's a beautiful, huge oil painting of the Charleston Harbor with big sailboats, waves crashing on the dock and seagulls flying above. It's sunset. The perfect evening in the Lowcountry.

I might go to jail and never see a harbor sunset again. I bury my face in my hands and try to take deep breaths to calm down. Our lawyer assured me that the hair isn't enough evidence to convict me, but the security cameras cause a problem. There also aren't any other leads beside me at this time.

"If you say you were home all night, the security footage would be your way out. But, it didn't break. You or Patrick turned it off willingly, which looks bad," Taylor had explained.

I need to talk to Patrick, but that thought scares me almost as much as the thought of being in a courtroom fighting for my life. A conversation like that could go south fast. I need to try and do some digging on my own first.

I sit up and make my way to my laptop. We had set up the cameras when we moved in years ago, so I open my email and begin searching my inbox. I finally find a welcome message from the company, asking me to verify my email address for the account. I click through the *forgot my password* steps, and finally I'm logged into our account.

There's a bunch of mumbo jumbo I have to filter through—payment information, camera features, etcetera—but I finally find a tab labeled "Activity Log." I click, and wouldn't you know it, I see all the times the cameras have been purposefully turned off by user PatMiller2014.

July 18, 2019.

July 22, 2019

August 8, 2019

August 17, 2019

September 1, 2019

September 8, 2019

September 28, 2019

October 5, 2019

October 22, 2019

November 14, 2019

...so on and so on, several times a month since July, ending with February 25, 2020, the day before Iris was found. Why would he want to turn off the cameras? I just don't get it. What reason would he have? After a moment, it suddenly hits me.

I raise my hand to my face and press hard on the bruise on my temple as I sort through the thousands of jumbled thoughts that are pouring through me. It's all making sense now. He had promised me it had been just that one time, and I stupidly believed him.

But now it was clear. It had happened dozens of times, maybe more, and he covered his tracks every single time. Maybe it wasn't just her. Maybe he had other women in his rotation.

The realization guts me. How could he? I pick up my cell and dial the contact number for the security company.

❀

As I shut the door quietly to Corinne's room after her bedtime story, I stand in the hall and try to gain enough courage to do what I need to do. Deep breaths. I squeeze my eyes closed. *You can do this*. I open my eyes wide and blink three times to focus.

I ascend the staircase to the third floor where my home office is. The plush white rug feels soft beneath my bare feet as I make my way over to the desk. It's a beautiful white painted wood desk with a flat screen desktop computer and various organization shelves and baskets for my papers. A large floor-length mirror is propped in the corner next to a white metal clothing rack. Patrick had set all this up for me when I started working harder on my blog. Before we had kids.

"I'm so proud of you," he had said to me as he kissed the top of my head, but those days are long gone.

I try to cling to those upsetting thoughts, the ones that will help me get through this. There's no telling how this will end, but I know I've got to go through with it. I have to save myself.

I open the bottom drawer and grab a small stack of papers that had been scanned to me earlier today. I already made copies and hid them, and I emailed them to myself too. Just in case.

"Okay," I breathe in a tiny, hushed voice. "I've got to do this now." I make my way toward the staircase.

"Patrick?" I ask as I appear in the doorway of the sitting room. He's sitting in his usual spot in his leather chair. He's just taken a swig of his scotch, and he looks over at me.

"Hey, Rosie. Come sit with me." He's in a good mood. He's got that look in his eye when he's feeling some tenderness toward me. He knows how to balance it out and to keep me hooked, waiting for these precious moments that make this joke of a marriage worth it, the moments that get me out of bed in the morning. But I'm not falling for it this time.

"I need to ask you about something." Why am I so nervous? I'm holding the evidence right here. He can't talk his way out of this one, and yet I'm still shaking in my lavender silk robe.

He doesn't answer, but looks at me annoyed, waiting for me to continue. He takes another sip.

"That night, when…when I found you with Iris. Th-that wasn't the first time you were with her." He keeps his narrow eyes on me, studying me. He's trying to see how much I really know. He wants to see if he can keep this up.

"You lied to me, Patrick."

CHAPTER 26

November 14, 2019

Charleston, SC

VIRGINIA

As I stare down at the black screen of my phone, I can't help but feel a little sympathy for this crazy girl.

Nella Rose had taken it upon herself to call me and apologize for the note and the shredded flowers, and it actually seemed genuine. Am *I* the crazy one for falling for this? I can't tell. I've been thinking about it nonstop since we hung up.

"Do you think I should believe her?" I had called and asked Bennett what he thought about it.

"I don't know. I still think we should have called the police. I don't like that she's just getting away with something like this." He's still on edge. He's not sure how to handle the girl drama.

But as I sit here—I've barely left where I've been perched in the kitchen since this morning—I realize something: it doesn't matter. This stunt of hers has shown her ass. One word from me about it to Iris, and she's toast.

But, there's the obvious problem. Iris knows about my obsession with her.

Plus, I didn't call the police like Bennett had wanted, so there's no proof. It would be Nella Rose's word against mine.

Who's she going to believe?

I could use this information I have against Nella Rose as leverage; she'd have to include me more because if she pissed me off, I could tell Iris what happened. Or, I could just tell Iris now and see if it freaks her out enough to drop Nella Rose completely and allow me to step in.

I slide my phone across the kitchen counter and put my face in my hands. I need to clear my head. It's time for a Plantation Meadows walk.

❀

I park my car in the usual cul de sac and start on my walk. It's colder now; I'm wearing thicker leggings and a long sleeve shirt with a puffy athletic jacket. The weather in Charleston is so random. A pretty intense cold front came in this week, and it feels like a true fall. I look up to the gray-blue sky and take in a deep breath. I love the cold.

I walk past my usual houses, being sure not to take any wrong turns this time. The woman in the green house has swapped her tennis skirt for a pair of impeccably tailored skinny jeans and a cozy ivory cardigan. Clutching a coffee mug, she's curled up on her porch swing. She waves at me and smiles.

Suddenly I find myself decidedly walking toward the entrance of the neighborhood, where I've never gone, and then I'm three houses down from Iris. Unlike Nella Rose's mansion and acres of land, Iris' home was a new build. The decrepit house before it had been demolished to build their new stunning four-story residence. There are about seven huge oak trees between me and her driveway. I can see John's silver G Wagon. In a normal neighborhood, houses are pretty much stacked on top of each other, but not here. It's a good distance walk from one house to the next.

Without realizing where my feet are taking me, I get closer and closer to her house, until I'm standing at the foot of the stairs, looking up towards her huge glass front door.

Why not pay her a visit? I could just say I wanted to come by to hang out for a bit. I can leave out the Nella Rose thing. We'll see where the conversation goes.

I can't text her because I left my phone in the car, so I go right up to the door and ring the doorbell.

To my surprise, John is the one who answers. He's holding Ivory on his hip, and he opens the door to greet me but looks strange. He's frowning, and as soon as the door is open enough he blurts out, "Virginia, where's Iris? Is everything okay?" He's looking over my shoulder like he should be able to find her there. Ivory is staring at me with her huge green eyes, and she wipes a purple substance from her hands onto her green plaid dress. She was wearing that on Iris' page this morning.

"Um, no. I…uh, just stopped by to say hi."

"She left an hour ago. She told me she was having dinner with you downtown." He looks even more worried now.

What? We didn't have any plans; I'm sure of it. I haven't talked to her in almost a week. Why in the world would she tell her husband she was with me? I try to rack my brain quickly, but my instinct is to go along with her lie and ask her about it later. She'd hate me if I ruined some kind of surprise she had for John, or whatever she was doing.

"Right! Uh, but I thought she said we were having dinner here. We must have misunderstood each other." I try my best to sound cheery, and from the relief on his face, he seems to buy it.

"Oh. Phew!" He's chuckling now as he sets squirmy Ivory on the ground. She runs off into the house to go play without a word. "I'm so relieved." He runs a hand through his blonde hair, which he keeps stylishly long in the front with a swoop to the side.

My goodness, this man is handsome. He also has bright green eyes (what are the odds that they would both have green eyes?) that dance above a proportionate nose, high cheekbones, and a strong, masculine jawline. They really are the most beautiful family I've ever seen.

I smile back, a little flushed. "Oh no, nothing to worry about." I feel the need to protect her, so I ask, "Can I use your phone to call her? I left mine in my car, and I feel so bad; she's probably been sitting at the restaurant waiting for me."

"Of course! Come in." John opens the door, and I step inside their house.

It's so colorful and fun. It's not as big and old-school Southern as Nella Rose's modern mansion, but it's much warmer. It feels like a home.

I follow John to their living room where he retrieves his cell from a white end table. He unlocks it and hands it to me.

"Here you go! Please save my wife from the embarrassment of looking like she was stood up!" He laughs.

I laugh back. "I know! Poor thing!" I take the phone and open his contacts, she has a purple heart emoji next to her name.

"Make yourself at home, I need to go find Ivory. She likes to hide when company comes over." He gestures for me to sit on the pink couch and disappears through the kitchen and out the back door.

I call her three times in a row before she finally answers.

"John, I'm sorry, sweetie, I told you I was at dinner with Vir-"

I cut her off. "Iris, it *is* Virginia," I say quietly to be sure John doesn't hear me. I can hear him cooing to Ivory on their back patio, patiently asking her to continue a story she'd been telling him about a squirrel.

"W-what? What's going on? Why are you calling from John's phone?" She's not irritated; she sounds panicked."I think you need to get over here. Like, now." I can hear the tone in my own voice change as I react to her shock and try to grasp what's happening.

She hesitates, then breathes, "I'll be there in two minutes."

Two minutes? Where was she? She must have been on her way home already.

❀

Iris and I are cuddled on her plush patio furniture on their back deck. John had installed a fire pit, and I sit there next to her, sipping my glass of Merlot, as she explains herself.

I am barely breathing. I don't want to miss one word.

"None of this was ever supposed to happen. You don't, like, plan this kind of thing, you know? It just…" She's staring in my eyes, pleading with me to understand. "One night, Nella Rose invited John and me over for a cookout. We all got pretty drunk on some kind of bourbon punch she had made, and I just kept finding myself looking over at him."

Patrick.

"He's just so *different* than John." She looks over her shoulder towards the house and lowers her voice. "He's like…a man. You know? He's blunt and always says what he means. He isn't a pushover. John just does whatever I say. It's boring sometimes." She pulls the fleece blanket up higher on her lap and reaches her hand up to her mouth. Her middle and pointer fingers graze her bottom lip as she recalls that night.

"I'm just…drawn to Patrick." Now she looks down at her lap, feigning shame, but I'm not convinced.

"I could tell John to dress up like a chicken and walk down Broad Street flapping his wings and he would do it," she says. She's almost whispering.

I'm studying her perfect face, and where I'm normally able to read her like a book, I'm struggling to figure out what this emotion is that she's feeling. It's almost as if she wants to feel bad about what she's done, but she's not able to.

It's as if she's ashamed of not being ashamed.

This is my opportunity, I think.

My mind is churning. I'm holding her deepest secret in the palm of my hands. She might not have meant for me to find out, but here I am, nestled on her fancy patio set while she spills.

I can't let this opportunity go to waste. I have to hold onto this. Keep her trust. Even if we are never going to be friends, holding a secret of hers like this will force a bond between us. I'll have the upper hand, and she'll have nothing of mine to hold over me.

Normally, if I would have found out a friend of mine was cheating on her husband with her best friend's husband (*wow, that's a lot to wrap my mind around),* I would have been, what?

Disgusted? I definitely would have felt compelled to expose her.

Inside their gorgeous home, with the warm and glowing light of a happy family, sits Iris' beautiful husband. He's probably putting their beautiful daughter to bed in her beautiful little girl's room. He'll walk into their beautiful bathroom, stepping heavily on beautiful marble tile, and curl up into their beautiful California King bed and wait for his beautiful wife to join him.

I have no idea what their marriage is like. Clearly, she believes he is falling short of her ideal, but as I listen to her talk about the way she feels about Patrick (*who has always been a bit of an ass, if you ask me*) I really start to feel bad for John. How bad can their marriage be that she has to wander down the road for random sex with a…what did she call Patrick, a *stronger* man? What does that even mean? John doesn't seem like a pushover to me. He just seems like a nice guy.

He actually has always reminded me a little of Bennett.

Crap. Bennett.

I suddenly remember I left my phone in my car. It's probably past ten, and Bennett has no idea where I am. It's very unlike me to be gone for this long with no explanation.

I can't leave though. Not yet. I've got to get her to spill it all. The more I know the better.

"You understand, don't you? You get where I'm coming from?" Iris' eyes are pleading. She needs me. I'm the only one who knows her secret, who can make her feel better about it.

"Of course I do, love." I reach over to grab her hand, and she gratefully accepts it. We look in each other's eyes. "Everything is going to be fine. We'll figure this out."

The whole Nella Rose thing is irrelevant now. I don't need to divulge that information anymore. This is so much better; and the best part is, it's something she'll absolutely never be able to tell Nella Rose.

This is just between us, and I'll sort through my feelings about it later.

CHAPTER 27

March 11, 2020

Mount Pleasant, SC

NELLA ROSE

"What did you say to me?" Patrick's body is frozen in place, but his face has taken a ghastly turn. He's been caught off guard, he's lost the upper hand, but he won't show any weakness until he knows what I have on him.

"You heard me, Patrick. I know about all the other times with Iris; it's all right here." I wave the papers in his direction.

"What the fuck are you talking about?" He looks annoyed, but he's eyeing the papers. I'll indulge him.

Walking over to the coffee table, I start setting out the papers one by one. They're scanned images, screenshots of video footage from the nights he turned off the cameras.

The only thing is, my *dear* husband bought an even better security system than he realized. After some research, I discovered that our particular package, one we pay $250 a month for, has a neat feature that records in a power-saving black and white mode with footage you can access in case of emergencies, even when you request them to turn off from your profile. The footage doesn't come up with all the other logs. You have to contact support, and they'll send over a file with all the footage that was recorded while your cameras were in "sleep mode." *Sleep mode*—not turned off. It's great for areas of the world where power outages are common, like here in South Carolina where hurricanes and tropical storms hit several times a year in the fall. The cameras don't actually ever turn off all the way.

"Sometimes robberies happen when there are power outages, like when customers evacuate for hurricanes, so this feature eliminates that issue," Brandy from customer service had explained to me over the phone this afternoon. "Our customers at this level of coverage are able to access every moment, and the logs are stored in our database for a year."

Detectives Marshall and Holliday must have overlooked this. It was only a matter of time before they figured it out, though.

Patrick doesn't get up, but his eyes are on the table. I've laid out 23 images of Iris leaving or entering our home at times when I was away. Most are just of her, some are of them together, but the most important one remains in my hands, the one of him leaving late that night. I try to stop them from shaking, but it's no use. My nerves are shot. I cross the room over to Patrick and gently hand over the image from the night of February 25, the night I had found them together.

The night before Iris was found dead.

I already knew about this night, but he had sworn to me it had only been that one time. For some reason, I had believed him. I had this bit of information stored away, ready to use if I really did end up getting arrested, but I hadn't been able to tell the detectives yet. If there was any way I could get out of this without humiliating myself and having everyone know Patrick was cheating, that's what I was going to do. When I thought the cameras were broken and there wasn't any proof of an affair, it was easier to keep quiet. But now, there were countless images of them together and a video of him leaving the house that night.

"You've been screwing Iris for MONTHS, and the night I find out about it, she dies." I'm surprised at my strength, but I clearly have the upperhand this time. "And then it shows you leaving and not coming back until the morning. It really was you, wasn't it?"

He throws himself up from his chair and snatches the paper from my hands. He shakes it in my face as he yells in his deep voice, "So *this* is your plan, huh?" He crumples the paper into a gnarly ball and throws it across the room as he continues. "You're not so smart, dear. If you took this screenshot from a whole video, yes it shows that I was...*with* her that night, but that it ended badly and with you in the middle of it."

My breathing is ragged. I find the courage to look up into his fiery eyes.

"Just say it. It was you, wasn't it?" I say as strongly as I possibly can.

"*Fuck you* for even asking me that! I may have gone too far with Iris, but I'm not a fucking murderer!" He's screaming now, and I reach up and press my hands against his mouth so he won't wake the girls but he pushes them aside. "If anything, you were so mad at her for betraying you that you just found a way to sneak out of the house, and *you* killed her! They found your hair!"

As he says this he pushes my right shoulder hard, and I stumble back against a chair. I knew the consequences of this confrontation but felt the need to talk to him first. This was stupid. I just needed to feel some kind of real power over him for once, but it's not working like I thought it would.

"It was your fault my hair was even on her! You got me into this!" Fire is pulsing through my body, giving me much-needed courage as it singes each vein. "And I wouldn't put being a killer past you,

Patrick. After all, you seem to have no problem hurting women."

He's really angry now. I can see his jaw clenching, his teeth grinding, his shoulders have tensed up and the veins in his arms are slowly becoming more pronounced. He's resisting his urge to attack me because he knows that isn't the solution this time. He can't beat me down.

Not unless he kills me.

CHAPTER 28

November 14, 2019

Mount Pleasant, SC

VIRGINIA

"Iris, your phone is ringing off the hook, babe." John appears from the back door and makes me jump from shock. I had been so deeply drawn into Iris and her story that I didn't hear the door open. His tall frame approaches us on the patio, hand extended, passing Iris's phone to her.

"Thank you, Johnny." Iris smiles as if her pretty head doesn't have a care in the world, and she takes the phone.

"You girls up to no good?" An effortless half smile raises the right corner of his mouth.

"Always." Iris gives him a playful look back, then directs her attention to the phone and John leaves us. Not a shred of doubt or worry seems to be on his mind. If only he knew the tales Iris had been recounting to me over the past few hours.

"Huh, I don't have this number saved." She scrolls through her missed calls."But they've called ten times."

It has to be Bennett.

"Can I see?" I ask as I reach over and she hands me the phone.

Yup, it's him. Oh no.

"Oh crap. Um, that's Bennett." I bite on the cuticle of my left thumb, a bad habit that stems from my anxiety problems. I don't have my medication with me. It's in my purse, in my car. With my phone.

"Does he not know you're here?" She looks concerned with a hint of judgment. That's ironic.

"Uh, well, it was sort of a last-minute decision to drop by. Do you mind if I call him back?" I unwrap myself from the blanket and stand up. This is a conversation that needs to happen in private.

"Course! You stay here, I'm gonna go inside and check on Ivory." She motions for me to sit back down as she rises in one graceful motion.

I nod, and after the door closes behind her, I take a deep breath and call him back.

"Bennett, I'm so sorry."

"*Holy shit*, Virginia, you're all right! Where have you been? Why aren't you answering your phone?!" He's out of breath, and it sounds like he's outside. I can hear the rush of cars in the background.

"I'm coming home, I'll be there in 15 minutes. I didn't mean to worry you." Try to stay cool. "Everything is fine; I'm at Iris'."

"Well, yeah, I figured that out." Bennett never takes this tone with me.

"Right. I'm so sorry, again. I'm leaving now."

❀

As I pull up to our house, I see Bennett sitting outside on the front steps. I study his face; I want to read him first. He looks angry. He's not worried anymore. He's frowning and watching my car as I put it into park and open the door.

"Bennett, baby, please forgive me. I'm really sorry for making you worry like that." I expect him to stand as I approach him, but he stays seated. He's just looking at me. So, I take a seat next to him on the cold bricks. There's a chill in this mid-November night, and I wrap my jacket tighter around my torso.

"How could you just disappear like that and not tell me where you were?" He's staring straight ahead at a tree across the street from our house. We face a beautiful park with a pond and lovely little wooden benches. There's a walking trail, which was a draw for us when we were deciding where to move. Bennett had said how nice it would be to have a place to walk Wilks. I've never used it.

"I was out everywhere looking for you," he says. Flat.

"I was on my walk, and I just decided to drop in on Iris. It was just going to be for a second, but…s-something happened." Make this about being a good friend; that sounds better. "She needed someone to talk to."

"What happened?" His voice is as cold as the brick beneath us.

"I can't tell you, B." I really can't tell him this. Can I? Will I shine brighter to him in comparison to such shady behavior on Iris' part? I guess, but I also can't be the one to air out a married couple's problems.

"Virginia, you need to tell me." He's looking at me now. "Because for the past five hours I have been sitting here thinking the worst had happened to you. You could have been dead. You owe me more of an explanation than that."

Our four brown eyes are looking at each other in a very different way than we ever have before. We've reached that point where we usually stop in every other difficult moment in our relationship. If we hadn't stopped in those moments before, maybe we could have prevailed. Maybe we could have moved forward and gotten even closer. For some reason, I always held back. I just said what I needed to appease him and move on with the fight, and he'd gone along just to bring peace to our chaos.

But now, I agree with him. I feel like I owe him the truth. And maybe through that, it can set me free a little more. Maybe I can release this hold I have on Iris and take on Bennett fully. Become a true partner, someone worthy of his love and affection and trust. I know I have it all in me, but I get distracted by the game of it all.

The winner of the game, of course, being the girl that everyone wants to be. Even someone like Iris. Would she maybe look at the relationship Bennett and I have and wish she could have that with John? Or is winning to her having her cake and eating it too? Having John, for everyone to see, and Patrick, in secret whenever she wants? Not just having her own perfect relationship, but also essentially taking that opportunity away from Nella Rose to have her own happy ending. Iris can laugh behind her back when Nella Rose says anything positive about her marriage.

I take in a swift breath and let it out slowly to settle my nerves. I need a second.

But I realize easily the answer is no. I'm not Iris. Perfect, for me, would be actually having the perfect marriage, the kind every little girl dreams about, not convincing everyone else that what we have is great yet behind closed doors it's a cold, dry wasteland.

No. I want the real thing. I need the real thing. I realize that that's really winning to me.

"I take walks in Iris' and Nella Rose's neighborhood, Plantation Meadows, all the time." He looks confused. A wrinkle forms above his nose as he tries to understand, but he stays silent and lets me continue.

"I walk their neighborhood three to four times a week." I sigh and look down at my knees. "I don't really know why; there's just something about being over there. So, when you asked me about running into Nella Rose outside her house before, I lied. I wasn't there to look at houses. I always walk Wilks there."

"Do you hope you'll run into Iris or something?" He's still wrapping his head around it.

"No, in fact, I usually avoid her street because I don't want her to see me there. It would be weird of me to be walking around over there. Tonight was the first time I decided to go by her house."

I won't tell him her secret, but I can tell him mine. Maybe he'll understand.

“It’s just, I don’t know. It’s the families in their grand houses. The perfectly paved streets. The young moms and their designer baby carriages. The couples with the lovely porches and plants. The manicured yards and fences with the pink rose bushes and the docks that lead to the ocean.” It’s just spilling out of me now.

“The fact that she lives over there in this perfect…bubble…I guess, I just…hoped that by spending some time over there, maybe some of its sparkle would rub off on me.” I’ve never actually said this out loud. “And if it did…maybe I would finally belong in her world. I guess I just don’t feel like I belong. I come from nothing, and I have nothing to offer them.”

“Virginia, I told you, we could move over there if we wanted to. We have the money.” He’s defensive.

“It’s not that. I promise.” He doesn’t get it. “If we moved there, both she and Nella Rose would think I was moving there just to try to be like them. They would think I was some crazy stalker trying to pry my way into the Flower Girls.”

"Virginia, do you know how crazy *that* sounds? Letting some stupid girls alter our decision on where to buy our house when you know how much I've wanted to live there? Do you really care more about what those girls think than…"

He won't finish that sentence. He's too embarrassed because he knows the answer to that. Deep down, he's always known that my end game pulls the strings. Iris is dictating my life. He's seen through my plan for a long time, but he lets his love for me and need to support me cloud his judgment. It used to be the perfect combination. It never occurred to me that he might have enough at one point.

"You cared more about being there for her tonight than how much I would worry from not hearing from you." He looks down at my ring, sparkling in the light of our porch lamp, sitting there on my finger making a mockery of him.

He's on the edge. I start to panic.

This is the moment, I can push past this invisible line we have drawn and tell the truth, or I can continue to tell him what he wants to hear just to keep him. Trick him into thinking he is happy.

Trick it is. We are eight months from our wedding, and I do love him. It might not be that true and honest love that he deserves, but it's all I can give at the moment.

"It was an aberration. I've never left you in the dark like that before. I promise, I never will again." I take his hand and let the tears fall. They're falling for him. How could I do this to him? The whole start of our relationship was a lie, and he'll never truly know his own wife.

But, I can promise to him and myself that I'll try harder. I can try to leave Iris behind and focus on him. I can try to cut the strings and make decisions based on what's best for us.

For him.

My life is not one short and fleeting puff. I need to think about who I might hurt. I'm not Iris. Maybe that should be my goal, to truly be better than her in every area. Even a much better person than her.

This is a good man, and he deserves to be happy.

"Can you forgive me?"

He looks at me hard, as if I'm a trivia question like the one on the TV shows we love to watch on weeknights.

"Yeah," he finally says. "But you have to promise me, no more secrets. I can't stand you doing things behind my back."

"Of course. I promise." I take his hand, and he lets me kiss his scruffy cheek.

"Let's go inside, babe." He stands and helps me up from the stoop and follows behind me through the door.

CHAPTER 29

March 11, 2020

Mount Pleasant, SC

NELLA ROSE

I clutch my ear as I stumble to catch myself on the back of the couch. Patrick backhanded me to the side of the head, not as hard as his usual blows. He's restraining himself. The last thing he needs right now is me showing up to the police station with these photos *and* a black and blue bruise on my eye. The big bad man who was cheating and beating on his wife.

This strike won't leave a mark, just a rattling in my head and a ringing in my ear. Maybe a little redness, but it'll fade after a few hours. I'm a pro. I can immediately tell by the force and location of a blow how much of a mark it will leave and how long it will last.

I look around the room through squinted eyes. The grand white marble fireplace. The navy blue upholstered couch. The eggshell paint on the walls trimmed with stark white stylish crown molding. The oak floors I try to keep steady beneath me. The antique Tiffany lamp perched on the side table. The diamond earring that has now pierced the skin behind my ear. With the throbbing pain beating in my skull with every heartbeat, I realize something.

I'm about to lose all of it.

He grabs my forearm and forces me to stand up straight and look at him.

"Nella Rose, you know you can't turn these in." He's steady. He's figured something out in his head.

"And what is that?" I narrow my eyes at him, more confident after his restrained hit, knowing he won't hurt me too badly tonight.

"Because. If I remember correctly, there's a blind spot in our cameras." He's looking even more devious as he releases my arm and takes a step back and leans against the fireplace. He crosses his arms.

"Remember, detective? The corner of the house by the dining room. Since there's only one window there, we decided that it wasn't worth adding another camera for just that one spot." He's looking positively cocky now. How does he remember that, but he doesn't remember the extra security features he added? I wonder how many times he snuck out to that exact spot. Is that how he knows?

"So while the backyard cameras might show you returning to the house after our encounter, you could have easily snuck out of that window and paid your dear friend Iris a visit, then returned without anyone the wiser." He's looking dead into my eyes. He tilts his head, like a puppy hearing an odd noise. "For all I know, that's exactly what happened."

"You…you look just as guilty as I do! You left and didn't come back until the morning and have *no alibi*! You slept in your car at the Point? Like anyone is going to believe that." I'm trying to stay calm. "And now that I know how many times you were with Iris, I'm sure there were plenty of others! That will make you look *so* good in front of a jury."

"Well, unfortunately for you, they won't have to," he says, evenly. "In fact, they're never going to have to hear anything from me. Except my testimony if they call me to the stand asking about you. Maybe you need to join Iris." With that, he pushes himself off the fireplace and comes at me.

I don't see his move coming but I'm quick and in good shape, so I dodge him and take off toward the kitchen. *Just make it to the back door.* He catches me and has me by the shoulder. I feel his body crash on top of mine, and we pile against our kitchen table with a clatter of wood against flesh, then flesh against marble floor with a terrifying slap.

"Why do you even…try to get away?" He's struggling to pin my arms down as I kick and thrash, trying to escape his hold, but he's much stronger than me. He presses a fist hard against my ear where he hit me moments ago. I feel like my head is going to explode from the pressure.

"You better quiet the fuck down before you wake our daughters," he hisses at me inches from my face.

As much as I want to scream for him to stop, I shut my mouth right away. He's not going to kill me. I just need to calm down so I can be free of his clutches and get my thoughts straight. I don't know what to do. I'm trapped. I should have just gone to the police with the screenshots and videos. Juries don't hang girls like me. I'm sure I'd be fine even if I was the only suspect. I made a huge mistake cluing him in; that's clear.

"You're going to keep that camera footage to yourself," he states as I slowly stop resisting. "You're fucked either way, with or without those videos, so you might as well leave me out of it, and I can take care of the girls instead of having both of their parents become suspects. You could also avoid publicly humiliating yourself by revealing how I was with Iris. For months. Right under your nose. She really did have everything you always wanted, didn't she?"

He must have felt my body freeze. I'm not fighting back anymore, that last verbal blow taking any remaining fight out of me.

"If you go to the police, I promise you, you'll regret it."

He's let go of my arms now, and I just lay there with my eyes squeezed shut. Like a roadkill possum, playing dead. If I stay still, he'll leave me alone. I can feel him lift his body off of mine, the weight from his strong, bulky figure slowly allowing me to pull in normal, deep breaths.

I notice how the cold marble feels good on my sweaty skin. My breathing slows as I focus on soothing myself. Wrapping my arms around my torso, I squeeze my eyes tighter and remember that night. I will let the fury give me my strength back.

CHAPTER 30

February 12, 2020

Charleston, SC

VIRGINIA

It's been a whirlwind of holidays and wedding planning. It feels as if I blinked and Thanksgiving, Christmas and New Year's Eve were gone, just like that.

Bennett's family came down from Tennessee to see us for Thanksgiving, and we traveled up to Georgia to see my parents for Christmas. Mom spent the entire three days gushing over how wonderful Bennett was and what a great match we made. Dad was glad to see us, but as usual, made himself scarce in their tiny house during our stay. He's always had a difficult time understanding this sparkly new world I've been living in with Bennett in Charleston. I can tell he's happy for me, but it's becoming less and less easy to relate to each other. Deep conversations are few and far between.

Now that I'm back home, I've returned to the daily grind with Bennett, and it's nothing but wedding planning with the big day coming up in June. Our tasting at the venue, a design meeting with the florist, rental shopping (how the hell does it cost $1,500 just to install some café lights?!) and budget meetings with the wedding planner. Valentine's Day is in two days, but we decided we were just too busy to plan anything big.

My mind whirls, thinking about all the to-do list items we have left as I speed down the highway to my dress fitting across town. I plan on losing at least ten more pounds before the big day, but I won't tell the seamstress that. I just plan on making one last fitting two weeks before I walk down the aisle so I don't look like I'm drowning in organza, and I'll look surprised when she tells me she has to take it in a few inches.

I can just imagine Iris saying, "Girl! Look at that tiny waist!" as she sucks in her cheeks to make a fish face, suggesting the appearance of my newly-pronounced cheekbones.

I'll laugh and say it must be from the stress.

I know Iris will be there, because she's been attached to my hip ever since our night together. She told the whole story of how it happened with Patrick.

Apparently, that evening at Nella Rose's house when they got bourbon punch drunk, Patrick had followed Iris to the bathroom, and he pressed her against the wall and they kissed right there against the fancy wallpaper that his wife had taken months to pick out. He had told her he couldn't stop thinking about her, and that things with Nella Rose were going steadily downhill.

"He promised me they were on the outs, that she was a terrible wife and that he was going to divorce her as soon as he could figure out the best plan for the girls," she had said as her full lips slightly curved into a smile.

I had risked everything to say this next thing, but I knew it was true. "Men always say that, and they never leave their wives, Iris."

I held my breath as I waited for her to snap a rebuttal to me, but instead she said, "I know, Ginny. I don't think he actually will. I would never leave John, either. He's the perfect husband and father. My followers would just die to see us separate, and it would be so humiliating. It's not like we could just all go our separate ways. Who would get to stay in the neighborhood? That's, like, ridiculous. I just need…a little…distraction every now and then," she said with a laugh.

Even though she didn't feel guilty about it, I still thought that since she was caught she would stop. I was way off.

In fact, now that she knew I could be her cover-up, I was getting texts from her about often asking me to lay low for the night and say I was with her if anyone asked. Anyone, of course, being Nella Rose. John wouldn't ask. He trusted her too much.

I had to admit, something about us sharing this secret made me feel like maybe this was a real friendship. She's coming over a few nights a week, or inviting me to her daughter's dance recitals, or asking Bennett to come along for double dates. And when we aren't together, she's always texting me.

How did the meeting with the caterers go?

You looked so cute in your post last night!

How's your morning going? You need to spill the tea on that green smoothie recipe!

For the first time, Iris has been treating me like a real friend. I wonder how different things would be right now if I hadn't decided randomly to go drop in on her at home during one of my walks. I wouldn't have found out about Patrick, and things would be exactly as they were before.

But they did happen, and now things are working just like I had wanted them to.

One step closer.

The only thing is, there was this thought I couldn't shake that maybe she could just be pretending to be my friend because I could out her. Of course, I have no proof of their adultery, but there's a chance Nella Rose or John would believe me if I told them.

As I pull up to the wedding dress boutique, I see Iris' Audi SUV already parked in the lot, waiting for me. Gravel churns under the weight of my tires as I pull into the spot next to her. I smooth my blue and white striped shirtdress and grab for my Neverfull.

"Ginny! I can't believe I finally get to see your wedding dress!" Iris squeals as she runs over to me and throws her arms around my shoulders. I breathe in her shiny hair, coconut and ammonia. She must have just gotten her hair touched up; it looks flawless.

"I know! Sorry I haven't shown you any photos." I release her embrace and lead her toward the entrance. "I wanted to make the big reveal in person." A tiny bell dings as we pass through the doorway and a heavyset saleswoman with perfect eyebrows and a news anchor voice greets us from the front desk. What's her name again? Something with an H? She stands from her desk chair and lifts her arms in a welcoming gesture.

She knows me by heart because I've been in here so many times. This isn't my first reveal; my mom drove down to see my dress weeks ago, and I brought two of my college girlfriends last week so they could see it with their bridesmaid dresses. I just wanted to give Iris a private viewing.

"Virginia, it's so nice to see you! Let's get you in your dress, shall we?" H-something leads me to the dressing room where I can see the hem of my dress peeking out the door.

"No looking until I'm in it, Iris!" I point to a chair across the room, telling her to sit and wait for me to get dressed. She eagerly listens and takes her place.

As I slip on the dress, I feel a rush of excitement and joy. It's such a cliché, but the whole big wedding dress reveal is definitely something I have dreamed about since I was little. Most girls do, I'm sure. It's been fun to do it so many times, and H-something hasn't said a word of opposition.

There's also another reason I brought Iris here alone today. I think through my speech as I stretch my arm into one of the dainty satin straps. Other than bonding us more by giving Iris a private viewing, I decided to ask her to be a bridesmaid today. Bennett had requested a last-minute addition and now we were uneven, so it was the perfect opportunity to add her.

H-something finishes zipping me up and gives me a second to look in the mirror.

"You ready?" she asks.

I nod, and she pulls the curtain of the dressing room aside for me to step through. I prepare myself for Iris' reaction.

"Oh, Ginny," she gasps. Her eyes are bugging out, and she draws a hand up over her mouth. Her green eyes are sparkling like the most dazzling emeralds as tears form then slowly fall down her cheeks. "You are the most beautiful bride I've ever seen."

Are those real tears? A wedding dress couldn't possibly warrant that type of instant emotion, could it?

Then, I watch as she puts her hands in her face and starts to sob. Like, really sob. The skirt of my dress swishes beneath me with every step toward her, and I kneel down to her level.

"Careful! There are pins!" H-something says to my back.

"Iris! What is it?" I ask as I grab for her hand. Her face is twisted up with pain, not emotion.

"It's…it…" She's trying to say something between gasps but can barely breathe.

"Calm down, calm down, it's okay. You can tell me. What is it?" I can't help but steal a quick glance down at the beautiful organza pillowing up around my knees.

As I look back up to her, she takes her hand from mine and wipes her eyes messily, not worrying about makeup. She looks at me.

"This sounds so terrible, and I can't believe I'm even saying this to you, especially here." She buries her face in her hands. Her emerald-shaped skating rink is twinkling in this brightly-lit room. What could she possibly not be able to say to me? She's told me everything, her darkest secrets of infidelity. What could be worse?

She shoots an accusatory look toward H-something, asking her without words to give us some privacy.

"I'll give you a moment. Just, please be careful with the dress, Virginia." Her bulky figure disappears behind a curtain in the back of the shop.

Alone now, Iris speaks.

"Please don't hate me for saying this. I just…sometimes wonder if…if my life is shit because I cheated on Bennett. I know it was a long time ago, but like, maybe all of this is karma. I have to live the rest of my life watching everyone else be happy. Like, really happy. And what do I get? Why can't I just love John like that? I think it's because I'm a bad person."

I stay kneeling as I process what she's saying.

She continues, "I mean, don't freak out; I'm not still into Bennett or anything. I just can't shake the feeling that no matter what I do, I'm just, like, defined by this one mistake I made a million years ago in college. I know, it probably doesn't make any sense, people cheat all the time, but…I don't know.

Ever since it's just, like, been a part of me. Even on our wedding day, I knew I wasn't going to stay true to John forever. It was only a matter of time. And now, I have this whole Patrick thing. I don't know what's wrong with me." She's not crying anymore, but I can tell that this is actually honest. No calculations.

"And I'll just have to continue watching more and more friends pick out their wedding dresses, have children, go on vacations, and actually *really* be happy."

She peeks through her slender fingers, and my silence encourages her to continue.

"I'm so sorry if this makes you feel weird, Ginny. I should have never said anything." With that, her face is back in her hands.

So, she honestly thinks that the karma of her cheating on Bennett in college years ago has forced her into a marriage with someone like John Sutten IV? Because of her mistakes, she's somehow bound to potentially ruin her marriage and other people's too?

What the hell?

I pull myself up and sit in the chair next to her, blankly staring in front of me as I try to think of what to say. Should I indulge her? Tell her everything is going to be fine? Or do I tell her how I'm really feeling?

Which is, obviously, I think it's awful what she's doing to John.

Even though I've had my share of doubts about Bennett. I go up and down on this rollercoaster of emotions like anyone, but I would *never* cheat on him.

If I'm being honest, I hate the way Iris treats her marriage like it's nothing.

She treats John like he's nothing.

If I didn't have the leverage to give me confidence, I wouldn't have had the courage to say this. But today, I do. I take a deep breath and look over to her.

"Iris." She looks over at me through puffy red eyes. "You can't let something that you did so long ago haunt you forever. Just stop seeing Patrick. If you really want to be happy, why don't you come clean with John? It's unfair to have this secret and live this lie. He might forgive you, and you can start over."

She's blank. She furrows her brow and breaks my glance, looking across the room for a second. I decide to keep going.

"Maybe you should even come clean with Nella Rose. You're not just ruining your own life, but also hers. Not to mention all your kids." I feel like that was a good enough speech to knock some sense into her.

"Wow, Virginia." No Ginny this time.

Shit. She's pissed. All the emotions that she had a moment ago were gone in a second, replaced by a terrifying look of anger. I've never seen her face like this. I feel my body subconsciously retreating away from her.

"You, *you*, of all people are going to judge *me*?" She grabs her YSL tote and pushes herself off the plush chair and towers over me. This is a power stance. I'm too freaked to try and stand up, so I just sit there stupidly in my huge dress craning my neck up to look at her.

"You just have all the answers, don't you?" Her face is stoic. The frilly and sweet-as-honey Angel Iris has been stripped away to reveal this Snow Queen.

"Do you *think* that you actually belong? That we would be *friends?* Yeah, right. Nella Rose and I might have our differences, but we are of the same kind. We belong in this world. We are what people actually want to be. And you," she looks me up and down, "how could I ever really be friends with you after you fucking stalked me in college? You want to talk about revealing secrets? Why don't we start there? Who do *you* think people will believe?" She's a rabid animal hissing every real thought and fear I've ever had, and I'm the scared little mouse. Cornered. Waiting to be devoured.

"You're sad. You're just a sad girl in a ridiculous, pathetic, off-the-rack wedding dress."

My heart has completely stopped. I didn't think she could possibly say anything else, but she continues, "The only real reason I have been hanging out with you so much is because I was afraid you would out me to John. But now that I know you're *so* worried about everyone's marriages, I guess I don't have to worry about that." She hisses but doesn't stop there.

"If I were you, I'd keep an eye on Bennett from now on. Men are men, *Ginny*, and he's already had a taste. I wouldn't be surprised if he came back for more one day when he's bored with you."

At that, she turns on her heels and swiftly makes her way across the store and out the front door. The bell sounds again, more like a toll than a chime this time.

I sit there and look down at my dress. The hem flows down from my hips to the floor like an icy waterfall, puddling at my feet as an ornate design of beading and pearls intertwine like frost across a frozen pond. I study the hand-sewn pattern so hard it almost looks like it's beginning to dance right in front of me. Tiny ice fairies are skating around in circles and curls, their wings sparkling and shining as they make their way up and over the hills of my knees.

I will my knees to unbuckle so I can stand. Smoothing out the fabric under me, I make my way toward the dressing room door as calmly as possible. I can hear H-something following behind me. She's clearly been listening.

"Can you please help me out of this?" I'm a zombie as she carefully unzips me and helps me step out of the dress.

CHAPTER 31

February 25, 2020

Mount Pleasant, SC

NELLA ROSE

I walk in the front door with my purchase from the liquor store, and I see Patrick out back hanging out with the girls. As I step into the kitchen, I notice the smell of garlic. He had put something in the oven for dinner. I'm tipsy, and it smells so good I might actually eat some of whatever it is. I go out the back door and call my family; the girls come running to me with sticky hugs, and I inhale their perfect smell.

He stands up and follows them slowly. I can tell by his face that he isn't happy.

I was late coming home, and I had forgotten to hide the new bottle of whiskey on the counter. It sits there, shining on the island under our pretty brass light installations. His eyes dart to the bottle through the big picture window then back to me. He looks me up and down and shakes his head at me.

"Mommy, we made mud forts!" Corinne chirps at me, and I look down at her perfect blue eyes. My baby. She's covered in mud, and her new lavender play dress is nearly ruined. Damnit, I haven't gotten a picture of her in that dress yet.

"Come wook, come wook!" Eleanor reaches up for me with her chubby hands, and I let her lead me into the yard, grateful for the delay in what I know is sure to come the moment I'm alone with my husband.

The rest of our night goes on like it always does—dinner, baths, bedtime stories and night-night kisses.

Then, as I slowly close the door of Eleanor's room, I feel a tug on my hair and I'm dragged down the hallway. I resist the urge to cry out so I won't startle the girls and let him pull me away from their doors.

"You've come home late and drunk too many times, Nella Rose." He spits at me, "You're pathetic. You know that, right?"

He still has my hair tangled in his hands as he pushes me against the bannister of our grand staircase, the one we had raved about together when we toured the house for the first time. He's ripping out pieces, detaching my extensions, and I can't help but let out a muffled cry from the pain.

"Oh, shut up." He pushes me off, causing me to stumble down two steps, but I catch myself.

"I'm getting out of here. I can't stand being around you another minute." He looks me up and down with disgust, then pushes past me on the stairs and storms out the front door with a slam. I slouch down on the stairs and hold my head, the pain finally catching up to me after the whirl of the adrenaline rush.

I sit there for a little while, but finally pull myself up and walk around in the darkness downstairs. From memory, I find my way to the bar cart and pour myself a drink, no rocks, and down it in one gulp. Burning liquid trickles from the corner of my mouth as I make another, crystal clinking against crystal. I drag myself to the sunroom.

Still not turning any lights on, I'm feeling at home in the darkness surrounding me. I find my usual perch and curl up into a ball. The sting of having my extensions yanked out is throbbing in a halo pattern across the back of my head. I reach up and touch them, assessing the damage and wince from the pain. Most of the pieces are still in there pretty well, but one small section feels like it's hanging on by a thread. How will I ever explain this to my hair stylist? It's not something I can fix myself.

I drink and wipe tears from my eyes, looking out the window at the full moon over the marsh. I consider what it would be like to step barefooted in the tall marsh grass toward the soft rippling waves of the ocean, to be eaten by an alligator or drown helplessly in the strong current.

Then something moves and catches my eye. A flash of motion. Like a small herd of white tailed deer. But it's too tall. Is that a person?

I spot another figure running across our backyard in the same direction, about 50 or so yards away, and one of our motion-detecting floodlights turns on. I study the yard, looking for the source of the movement, but can't find anything. Our huge oak trees that frame the dock blow gently in the evening breeze, and I can see the Spanish moss sway in the artificial glare of the floodlight.

My pulse starts to quicken. *What was that?* My eyes are glued to the spot behind the tree where I had seen the figure disappear. Then, I see the other figure. Two figures, together. Pressed up against a tree. They're entwined. Kissing? I can almost feel my heart stop completely.

It's Patrick. I can see his shoulders and the curve of his face, and in the dim glow of the floodlight, I realize who's there with him. I'd recognize that perfect hair and tiny waistline anywhere.

It's Iris.

He's hiking up her skirt as she wraps her leg around his waist. His hands are all over her, and her lips are on his neck. I can't take my eyes off of them. I stare in disbelief, then something inside me snaps. His words repeat in my head, "This isn't what I signed up for…"

Of course. I'll never measure up to her. She's the ideal. I wasn't enough, so he finally snapped and decided to move on to someone better. His angry blows had become more frequent, and his disgust was building. Of course I had thought this was a possibility.

And Iris? She was supposed to be my friend. She listened to me talk about how awful Patrick could be. She knew all of that, our whole story, and still has the nerve to come to my house and screw my husband in our backyard where our kids play?

I can't look away. My rage is being fueled by the sight of them together. I shakily set down my drink, and before I realize what's happening, my feet are carrying me to the back door.

I'm full-on fearlessly drunk now as I stumble across the yard. They must have heard me coming because they've jumped away from each other and are fixing their clothes. Iris pulls down her skirt and runs her beautifully manicured fingers through her hair. Patrick is zipping up his jeans. Even in this dim light, I can see the looks on their faces. A complete lack of an escape plan.

"How could you." I'm looking at her, not Patrick.

"Nella Rose, please. He…he told me y'all were separating," Iris begs.

And now she's going to lie to me? She saw my post just today of the two of us, a photo I had taken weeks ago when we were having a good day. She had commented on it, *How cute are you two*?!

She's standing there, shaking. She has to be cold in this ridiculously tiny tennis skirt. It's dropped down in the 50s on this late February night.

"Don't lie to m-me." My words are slurring. I'm starting to see double. As if two of this perfect human needs to exist.

I take a few steps forward. Patrick is standing firm, silent, but Iris takes an unsteady step back. We stand there for a second, staring at each other. Her green eyes are pleading. She looks sorry, but I don't care. I won't let her get away with this.

All this time I spent trying to be her friend, and all she did was fuck me over. She ditched me for

Virginia, and now she was taking my husband? It's too much for me to stand.

I lurch forward and try to tackle her to the ground, but she is sober and has about five inches on me, so she stands firm against my blow.

"You...you *bitch*! How could you do this to me?!" I try to slap her, grab her, but she's reading all my moves before I make them. I hear the jingle of her thick purse chain as it swings around us in our tussle. I'm unsteady and a step behind, and suddenly it's me falling to the ground from my own violent attempts instead of her.

I feel a sharp pain in the back of my head as I go down. I hit the grass beneath the oak tree. I can feel the grass and dirt on my palms, moist and cold in the evening dew. All my movements are delayed, and by the time I push myself up to look at her she's already running off. I see something following behind her, bouncing off her hip and blowing in the wind as she disappears around our house. I reach up gingerly to my head and feel the place where the chunk of extensions Patrick had ripped loose is missing.

CHAPTER 32

March 12, 2020

Mount Pleasant, SC

NELLA ROSE

I stare out the window at a great blue heron standing still in the marsh. It's barely 7:00 a.m., but I haven't slept all night. Sometime early this morning when Patrick left, I dragged myself to the couch in the sunroom and curled up into a ball, trying to calm down.

When Patrick had finally been convinced that I wasn't going to reveal the security footage of that night to the detectives, he was out the door. I don't know where or when he'll be back. Maybe he'll never come back. A girl can dream.

I've never been so afraid of my husband. Every other time he had laid his hands on me like that, it was always somewhat minor. A push here, a shove there. The extensions were the worst up until now.

This was the first time he'd threatened to kill me. I could see it clearly now. Any shred of love he had for me is gone. For good.

What can I do? I wonder. I reach my hand up to my ear and wince as I feel the tenderness of the bruised skin. I take my diamond earring out and cup it in the palm of my hand. Its sparkling beauty is laughing at me. I'm a fucking joke.

This is what all of this has been for? I ask myself as I stare down at the perfectly-cut and clear 5-carat stone. Something comes over me, and all of a sudden I'm rushing to the back door and throwing open the large French doors. My bare feet carry me across the yard through the oak trees toward the marsh. The sunrise is just coming up over the water, sparkling like a million 5-carat diamonds in orange morning light. A creamsicle dawn. This is my favorite time of day. The colors are so soft and fluffy; I can almost feel them. I want to hold them in my hands, cup them, like you would a fallen baby bird.

The raw and rough wood of the dock is a striking comparison to this light. It pokes up at my bare feet as I run, on and on until I've suddenly reached the end. The wooden railing hits me in the stomach as it stops me from toppling into the salty water. Tears are streaming down my face. I didn't think I had any left.

Looking down in my hand, I remember the diamond earring. I reach up to my other ear and remove its partner, clutching both. I squeeze tight and feel the back of them poking into my palm, this little $500,000 gift Patrick had bought me for Christmas the year after we got married.

I had worn these and looked around at all my nice things over the past six years, trying to remind myself that this was worth it, that I could take his blows to my body and mind. That showing up to a brunch in the most expensive dress or driving around in the nicest car or having the biggest house in the neighborhood simply came with a price. I remember thinking many times that it could have been a lot worse. One in four women experience domestic violence, and yes, I was one of them, but at least I was rich.

These earrings represented it all to me. The abuse was like a tiny white paper price tag hanging off the back of these earrings in the jewelry store. Patrick was offering me this life, and all the beautiful sparkling details I'd be able to possess, all with the price of him being in complete control of it all. I'd been willing to pay it all this time, but not anymore. I won't be the fool anymore.

With a swift motion, I throw my consolation prize into the ocean with all the strength left in me. With a tiny and insignificant plop, they break the surface of the water, and I imagine them slowly sinking down and resting on the sand below with all the other lost and forgotten dreams.

The girl who had worn those 5-carat lies is gone. It's time for her to write a new story of her own.

I turn away from the rising sun and make my way back toward the house.

❀

"Where are we going, Mommy?" Corinne is secured in her car seat, squirming around in her purple flannel pajamas while Eleanor sleeps in her seat next to her.

"I'm sorry it's so early, button," I coo, hoping I haven't startled them too much. "I just have some errands that couldn't wait until later."

I'm driving really slow as I make my way toward the station where Detective Jehli and Detective Holliday will be waiting for me. I'm fighting the old Nella Rose every step of the way as she urges me to forget it all and go back home, but I won't. As I roll up to a stop sign, I steal a glance over to my open Prada riding in my front seat.

Patrick hadn't destroyed all the screenshots of the video footage I'd printed. After he laid me out on the floor and quieted me, he had gone upstairs to my desktop computer and cancelled the security membership. He requested a permanent delete on any and all footage that had been collected during our use of the service and checked my files to see if I had saved them anywhere. He's not thinking straight either, because obviously this would make him look more guilty, I would think.

Luckily, I was prepared for this. The day I had found the footage, I had sent the files to my blog email, which he doesn't have access to. There, in an email to myself, attached under my curly-Q cutesie blogger email signature, were all the black and white files showcasing their affair, and. of course, the one of our fight, showing how my hair got stuck in her purse.

I printed more screenshots from the video after Patrick had thrown the ones from last night in the fire, and they peek out at me from my purse. The image facing me is one from November, of Iris blowing Patrick a kiss from our driveway as she's leaving our house.

On the phone, the detectives hadn't said much to me other than to tell me to pack overnight bags for me and the girls.

I figured that. Suddenly, Patrick is now going to be seen as a violent person, and while he has never hurt the girls, there's no telling what he might be planning to do, just in case I did find the courage to leave. He has the money and resources to have them gone and untraceable in a second. And I know he would do that just to hurt me more.

The decision to reveal the cameras means our world is about to change forever. The girls will have to go through having either their mother or father face trial for murder and the reprocussions of a nasty and public divorce.

I am leaving my old life behind. And if I ever do step back inside the grand entryway of that house, it won't be as the wife of Patrick Miller. Our marriage is over, and I am finally free of him.

CHAPTER 33

February 25, 2020

Charleston, SC

VIRGINIA

It's been almost two weeks since I've spoken to Iris or Nella Rose, but I see the Flower Girls dancing across my feed every day. Sometimes alone, sometimes together, always looking flawless and happy.

Two weeks ago, it would have been me.

Definitely not anymore.

Iris had done something, started some kind of digital war against me with her followers, and I guess Nella Rose followed as usual. I don't know how they did it, but ever since the fight between me and Iris at the bridal shop, every time I post something I get hundreds of hate messages and comments.

You're such a bitch! Iris is the best human in the world, leave her the fuck alone!

You're just jealous because you're not as pretty as her!

No one gives a shit about you or your wedding. Why don't you just disappear?

And so on and so on. Hundreds of them. Thousands even? I've stopped trying to count.

They must be spreading some lies or rumors about me, saying that I'm bullying Iris or something, and her very loyal followers are tearing me to shreds. She's got a lot of influence. Everyone loves her, and her dedicated fans have become her warriors. I'm the target.

I haven't posted in over a week because I just spend hours deleting the messages and blocking the people writing them. But even when I don't post, they still come flooding in. Some people are even texting me. She must be giving out my number too.

Bennett is cuddling me on the couch and watches me as I watch my phone light up with message after message on our glass coffee table. They're nonstop tonight. I had the audacity to post some stories of me and Bennett going to get drinks tonight, and I'm getting a new reply from an Iris follower every few minutes.

Oh, wow look at you two, the couple who will never be as cute as Iris and John.

Why are you even a blogger? You're like, fat. You know that right?

Wow, another entry in the boring life of Vanilla Virginia.

As much as they hurt, I still keep thinking I could have come up with better insults.

"Baby, just turn it off. It'll stop eventually." Bennett reaches over for my phone jokingly, but holding onto it tightly is my instinct.

"You don't know that, Bennett. I get torn apart every time I post. It's only a matter of time before enough accounts report me or something and my account gets removed completely." I shrug him away and move to the opposite end of the couch. Wrapping my oversized cardigan sweater around me I stare into the fire, blindly avoiding his eyes.

"All the time and work and stress. It will all have been for nothing." My voice is robotic and matter-of-fact, but the fear begins to choke me as I let that thought sink in. It's been years since I've allowed myself to even consider the possibility that I might not have the life I pictured for myself. That I might do something different. What if I just wasn't cut out for it?

Maybe it's over. This could be a sign for me to give it up.

If I was supposed to make it, wouldn't I know by now? Wouldn't one thing have come more easily for me? Or, maybe there's a reason why this class system exists. No one is allowed to break it. The self-made are labeled as such. No matter how high they might climb, the whispers of the old money rich would continue to echo throughout the neighborhood, "We've been here all along. No amount of money puts you in the same class as us."

Tom Buchanan and Jay Gatsby. Old money and new.

We might have traded pearl necklaces with Gucci bags, but has that much really changed? Other bloggers might deal with the class system purely in terms of followers and monetary success, but my goal has always been much bigger than that. I wanted it all. I wanted these old money rich girls to consider me one of them.

Bennett isn't giving up tonight. He sets down his wine glass and makes his way toward me, cornering me on the couch. His compassion warms me a little.

"Virginia, I know there's no real way for me to understand what you're going through. Okay? I get it, but this is just getting out of hand. Maybe we should just move. You know, pack up everything and try another city. We could have a fresh start in Nashville or Austin or wherever you want to go." His big hands gesture across the living room as if to show me the endless possibilities out there.

I steal a glance at him. His offer sounds so promising, but I can see the torment in his eyes. There's a battle going on in his head underneath that tousled head of hair. I know he would rather stay. He loves it here; he's told me a million times how he wants to live here until retirement, and he doesn't exaggerate. But he also doesn't offer false promises. He means it.

He would do it for me. He would start over if it would make me happy.

"Do you think that could be the answer?" I can't believe myself as I say the words. "Would you really do that for me?"

His eyes widen. I don't think he was expecting me to accept that offer. I'm honestly shocked that I'm letting myself consider this, but as I think about the opportunities another place could bring me, it's sounding better and better. New people. New friends. I could get a job in marketing or something, where after 5:00 every weekday I could do whatever I wanted to do.

I could go thrift shopping again. I wouldn't have to worry if every piece of furniture we buy is going to be in stock online long enough for me to post about it. I wouldn't have to spend hours of my vacations making Bennett take photos of my outfits.

But there were also so many good parts about blogging. If I took Iris and Nella Rose out of it, I had really met so many nice girls through it. I've been able to travel all around the world, go to fabulous parties and events, meet celebrities, and get lots of free clothes, shoes, bags, you name it. It used to be so fun. I remember feeling really lucky in the beginning to do what I do. Why did I let it all change?

"Of course, I would. It would be a fun change for us. We could figure it all out right after the wedding," he says. "Whatever we have been doing here for the past year, it isn't working anymore. Something's gotta change."

"Are you talking about us?" I say. A different kind of panic hits me hard like a brick wall. "Because, I thought you wanted to do this just to help me get away from those girls so I could be happier. I didn't realize you thought things weren't going well for *us.*"

"No, no. I mean, well…we were just a lot happier when you weren't so stressed about all this." He glances down at my phone. "I know it's not your fault, but I just want us to be close again. Like we used to be. We're about to get married, you know? I just want us to be good."

I knew that I'd been in more bad moods, but I had no idea it was making him doubt how he feels about me. "You know, Bennett. Life gets stressful sometimes, so sorry I can't be perfectly cheery every day."

He reaches for my face with tender urgency and says, "You know that's not what I mean. Of course, you're allowed to have days when you're upset. But don't you *want* to be like you were before? I just want you to be happy. This job used to make you happy, and it just doesn't anymore, that's all I'm saying. And I think we both know that it's not the job, it's them." Of course he means Iris and Nella Rose.

As much as I want to believe him, my mind is now a complete tornado. I'd been struggling in other areas, but I always had Bennett. And now I can feel him slipping away from me.

"I'm going for a walk," I say as I rise from the couch and make my way toward the bedroom to change. It's still chilly at night, so I grab my puffer jacket from our closet and throw it on over my sweater and swap out my ripped denim for some hunter green leggings. Sitting on the edge of our big bed, I begin to lace up my sneakers.

I can hear the rustle in the other room as Bennett follows me to the bedroom and stops in the doorway. He leans against the frame, watching me fumble with my laces, trying to look casual by crossing his arms. I'm watching him from the corner of my eye. I can read his next move before he even speaks.

"Baby, it's so late. Why don't you just wait until morning?" He's been weird about my walks ever since the time I was at Iris' so late. He's trying to keep his voice steady, but I feel the pleading edge of it from across the room. He's not going to force me to stay; that's not his way. He'll let me go if I push past him.

I stand up from our bed and head to the bathroom to find a hair tie. I actually know there is one in my car, but I'm just stalling. I don't really want to leave so late. Looking in the mirror over our his and her sinks, I slowly begin to pull my heavy locks into a long braid at the nape of my neck. My fingers habitually loop the dark strands over and under each other down and over my shoulder until they come to an end at my waistline where I tie them all together. I look up and see Bennett's reflection in the mirror over my shoulder, still in his place in the doorframe. He's looking down at his feet. He's defeated.

The Virginia that he's been dealing with over the past year would brush by him without a word, get into her car, and drive off to Plantation Meadows despite his pleas for her to stay.

That Virginia is selfish. She knows that she can do whatever she wants, and he'll still stick around.

But now, I don't know. I might be losing him. The one thing in my life that has made any sense at all lately might be slipping out of my grasp.

What is wrong with me?

I press both my hands to my face and start to cry. I can't help myself. Tears start pouring down my cheeks. I can't even think. I just let this overwhelming feeling absorb into my skin as I drink it up and let it pour back out of me.

I feel Bennett wrapping his big arms around me and holding me tight. I feel his strength. This answer is here, not on some street in Plantation Meadows and definitely not on my phone. There's so much I can't control, but I can fix us.

I turn around to face him and bury myself in his embrace. We stand there, holding each other for a long time.

I push off a little so I can reach up and kiss him. It's just him and me. The swirling and sinister world out there does not exist in this home right now.

He peels off my jacket and grabs my waist to lift me up on the counter. His powerful hands move down and clutch me tightly at the fold where my hips meet my thighs, his thumbs cuppings my hip bones with purpose as he presses himself between my legs. I run my hands through his hair and lock his lips in place against my own.

These kisses are like the kind you have when you first start dating someone. Forceful and intense, like you both know where you want it to lead but you just haven't gone that far yet and you're not sure who is supposed to make the first move. After a while, the kisses usually become a brief start to foreplay just to lead to the end result, but tonight we're staying here for a moment. I can feel his heart beating wildly against my chest as we press ourselves further into each other.

Gently, his hand on my neck, he pulls me away and stares straight at me. I've never seen this look of his before.

"Stay," he says. It's not a question.

"Okay," I breathe. I feel his hands reach under my thighs as he lifts me from the sink and carries me to the bed.

CHAPTER 34

March 12, 2020

Mount Pleasant, SC

NELLA ROSE

I wave to my mother from the curb of the police station as she drives off with my babies. She made the drive from Rockville in her little gray sedan, and she's taking them to a nice hotel in downtown Charleston. I had made a hefty withdrawal from the bank on our way here so she could pay in cash.

I don't know what Patrick plans to do, but he's staying far away from the girls until this is figured out, and I can't have him tracing the credit cards to find them. They aren't leaving the state or anything, so it doesn't look like I'm "kidnapping" them from him. If he asks, I'll tell him. I'm just going to avoid his calls so that he can't.

"Let's go inside." Detective Holliday motions for me to follow her back into the station. I look over to our lawyer. Taylor Wright didn't hesitate when I explained to her over the phone this morning that I'd need her here with me today. I had explained the complicated nature, and how Patrick might wind up being on the opposite end of me and that she'd be representing me alone, but she said it was all right.

"We can't let them get away with this kind of thing, Nella Rose. I'm going to protect you from him," she had said.

Taylor gives me an encouraging nod, and we both follow Detective Holliday inside. Here we go.

We take a seat in the same room as before, and the same four people are present, but things are very different this time. My child's chair squeaks as I take a seat, and I look over at Marshall and Holliday across from me at the table. The officer is sitting in the corner again, only this time, he's looking slightly less bored.

Marshall steals a glance at Holliday, then decides to be the one to begin.

"Nella Rose, I understand you have some information you'd like to share with us."

No kidding. "Yes, I do." I've gained so much confidence through all of this. The fear of being back in our home with Patrick is scarier than any prison cell. Whatever happens in this room, I know I can handle it. I'm stronger than the girl who sat here before.

I grab for my Prada and pull out the stack of screen shots and hold them in my hands. *This is it. I can do this.*

I exhale and slide them across the table for the detectives. I'd written in black marker the dates and times each one was taken.

"I've discovered that I don't know Patrick at all. He had been having an affair with Iris for months without my knowledge." I look down as a moment of shame passes over me, but I brush it off quickly and look up at them again. I will not let him make me feel this way. He's the one who screwed up. I didn't screw up.

I go on to explain the camera features, how he thought he was turning them off but that they were still filming, then I go into the night of the murder. I spare no detail on the beatings and the way he yanked out my extensions.

"I caught them screwing right in my backyard. I confronted them, I actually tried to fight her, and that's when my hair got caught in her purse. I was too afraid to tell you about that night because I know that it sounds bad, but I'm telling you, I didn't kill her."

I point to the photo of Patrick leaving later that night. Taylor notices me getting emotional so she takes it from there.

"Mr. Miller told my client after their altercation that he was going for a drive. He left the house here," Taylor says as she points to a series of photos, "and here he is returning the next morning. He said he got tired, so he pulled over and spent the night at the Point. His Find My iPhone had been disabled as he had done many times over the past year. Looking at his phone records, you can see that most of the times he disabled it correlate directly with the dates of the camera shutdowns.

"I'm sure you have been battling privacy laws trying to get access to their footage, but I assure you, Nella Rose has nothing to hide. It should also be known that Patrick cancelled their security membership, thinking that it would delete everything, but I have been in contact with the company and will work with you on gaining full access if need be."

I sit and listen as Taylor goes on, stating all the facts more eloquently than I could, but I can't help but choke down horrifying panic. They probably already know about the blind spot. They're probably just sitting across from us letting us go on and on, only to slam us some evidence negating everything we had. Patrick could be here right now. He could have sweet-talked the detective hours before I got here.

He could be watching me from the other side two-way mirror.

Taylor pauses and looks toward me, "Also, Nella Rose has never reported her violence before, but today she would like to."

I glance at Taylor, but as we had discussed on the phone, I pull my hair back and turn my head to show the detectives the red mark behind my ear. Next, I pull up my blouse sleeve to reveal a hand shaped bruise on my right arm. I'm shaking all over.

"Thank you for telling us, Nella Rose. I know how hard this must be for you, but you're very brave for reporting this. We will take some photos and file a full report after this interview." Marshall gives me a look of encouragement.

The room is dead quiet for a moment when suddenly Holliday's phone violently buzzes, startling me.

"Detective Holliday....yes...mmm-hmm...okay..." She pauses for a few moments, listening to the person on the line. Then, she looks up directly at me. "Yes, well. Thank you for that information. We'll be in touch. Goodbye."

"Well, that was Patrick's lawyer. He received word from Patrick that you are unstable and have taken your children without his knowledge. He says that you might hurt yourself intentionally to frame his client for abuse." Holliday sets her phone down and interlaces her fingers on the table. "Also, he mentioned something about a blind spot in the cameras, and a problem with alcoholism."

No no no no no. He can't do this to me.

In my panic I blurt out, "Of course I didn't do this to myself! Look at everything he's done, *it's him*! He's a liar and a cheater and has hurt me so many times," I continue, my hands shaking violently as I try to clasp them on my lap. "How can you believe him over me? I haven't done *anything*! And, yes, the girls are with my mother, but I was afraid he would hurt them too or take them away from me! *I'm scared*!" Tears are pouring from my eyes and I can't stop them.

I turn my attention to the table and shakily point to the two images of the backyard and the side of the house, showing where the window is that isn't caught on camera. Tears flooding my eyes, I continue, "And…and yes, even though there's a blind spot on the camera, the other cameras show that I never left the house after I came back inside. I would never leave the girls in the house alone no matter how upset or…drunk I was!"

Marshall continues to examine the photos, but Holliday looks up at me. It's a different gaze than the ones she's given me during our encounters over the past few weeks.

She's going to tell me the worst, I can feel it. My heart sinks lower and lower. Patrick has a whole case against me, now. Of course he planned on framing me as an unreliable source. My drinking doesn't look good, and it wouldn't have been difficult to make that mark on my head myself.

"I know there's no proof I was home, but please believe me. I didn't do this. Patrick is lying. He's *lying!*" I'm pleading.

Holliday brings her hands together on the desk as if in prayer. She studies me for a second with a narrowed brow before she speaks.

"Nella Rose, we need to find Patrick. Do you know where he is?" Her eyes are big, and I can tell her mind is churning. Is she thinking about the trial? Deciding which of the Millers to send to court?

"I don't know; he left again last night. He hasn't tried to contact me. Did his lawyer say anything?" I look down again. I should have called the police last night and gotten his beating on record earlier."Do me a favor." Holliday slides the image of Patrick leaving out the front door the night of Iris's murder. "Look at this photo carefully and tell me what you see."

I do as she says, taking the image in both hands and bringing it close to my face to study it. It's a shot of Patrick's back as he's locking the front door. *That's ironic*, I think. I'm not afraid of thieves in the night. What I'm most terrified of can enter and leave this house as he pleases.

As I look closer, though, I see he's wearing a backpack. That's odd, since he claimed he didn't plan on staying out all night, but that's not the only thing that catches my eye.

Sticking out of the mesh side pocket of the backpack is his revolver. I can barely make it out in the grainy black and white image, but it's there. No mistaking it. It's shiny metal gleams in the porch light. It's an antique, passed down from his great grandfather.

I stare at it for a second.

"He…but she…Iris wasn't shot, right? I thought she was…strangled." I continue to stare at the revolver. It's the one he kept in the gun safe under his side of the bed to protect us.

"Yes, she was strangled." Holliday states. "But the fact that he left that night with a weapon is more than enough evidence to take him to trial. It proves an act of violence was premeditated. He could have confronted her with the intentions of using the gun, then realized he couldn't lure her away from the earshot of her family and the neighbors, so instead he chose a… quieter method."

I look into her blue eyes without a word. She blinks heavily mascaraed lids at me.

Marshall steps in with her intake, nodding her head in agreement. "Yes, exactly. And with his whereabouts being completely unknown during the time when Iris was murdered, it's enough for an arrest. Add in his violent behavior against you…"

She lifts her hand and taps her ear in the spot where Patrick struck me last night. "I don't know what jury would let him get off for this. I know he has the resources to get the best lawyer in South Carolina, and it might be too early for me to say this, but I think what we have is enough to beat him if this goes to court. The whole *he said she said* approach in terms of violence against women isn't holding up the way it used to."

I haven't taken my eyes off of Holliday as I take in Marshall's words. She reaches across the table, and I put down the photo to take her hand. This is the warmest gesture she has ever given me, I realize, as she squeezes my hand. I feel my wedding ring cut into the sides of my surrounding fingers.

For some reason, my wedding ring has never felt like a symbol of our marriage. When Patrick proposed, I was genuinely very surprised because he had never asked me what kind of ring I had wanted. Usually, you send your friends photos or leave tabs on your computer open "accidentally" with ring ideas from Pinterest when you think you're about to get engaged, but Patrick had never asked my friends, and he proposed only eight months after we met. I never saw it coming. He picked out the ring himself, a 6-carat, rare Fancy Pink oval diamond nestled in a starburst design of diamonds on a plain platinum band. It's so big and obnoxious that I only wear it out when I'm trying to impress people, and I knew he only got it because of the price tag, $618,000. The price of a nice house. Well, pretty nice, I guess.

I don't like pink diamonds. That sounds like something some ungrateful rich bitch would say, but it's true. I think they're silly. I would have wanted something classic. When he presented me with that ring, something inside of me clicked. He didn't know me at all.

I got myself into this. I knew he was sort of a jerk from the beginning, but I ignored all the red flags because I was determined to have a certain kind of life, and he was the key. His status, his money, the mansion, the cars, they were all going to be mine. It was never discussed, but I knew after he presented me with that ring that he was using me too. I was a doll to him, something to give expensive gifts to that would show off how much of his fat bank account he was generously spending on his pretty little wife.

All I had to do in return was play the part, and when I failed, he punished me for it.

My ring has always felt more like a business partnership, one that I entered into willingly, which is why it has such a different meaning to me. The earrings were given to me after our first big fight, about a year into our marriage. The first time he laid his hands on me. I'll never forget the way it felt. We were hosting a dinner party for a few of his work friends and their wives, a celebration of Patrick's promotion, and I had made a joke at his expense. It was harmless; I don't even remember what it was because he had hidden the fact that I had upset him so well that the moment doesn't stand out in my head. After our guests had left, I was standing, collecting long-stemmed champagne flutes on the marble island, when I suddenly felt him grab me by the shoulder and turn my body roughly to face him.

He squeezed his large hand, which spans from the tip of my shoulder blade up to my collar bone, so hard it felt like his fingers were going into my flesh. I cried out, but he took his other hand and grabbed my throat and told me to be quiet.

He said something along the lines of how I had humiliated him in front of everyone and made a fool of myself, and that if I was going to be his wife, it came with certain rules. I stood there silently, his hand not really squeezing my throat, just gently clutching it at the base as a warning of what could come. He asked if I understood, and I nodded.

I was five months pregnant with Corrinne at the time.

The next day, as I was preparing dinner, he came home from work and presented me with the earrings. He begged me to forgive him and promised he would try to control his anger. I believed he would try and accepted them. Yes, he had hurt me, but he was paying me back for it and promised he wouldn't do it again.

I had held on to those earrings as a symbol of something. I still can't make sense of it completely. I don't think of myself as one of those stupid girls you see in the movies, staying as their husbands hurt them. I don't see it that way because their relationships were different than ours. I had entered into this marriage with just faint feelings of love and more strong feelings of self-preservation. The earrings meant he was holding up his end of the bargain, so I wore them every day as a reminder of why I was there. Less happy marriages exist under much worse circumstances, I would remind myself. I could be with someone who truly beats me, broken ribs and kicks to the gut. And I could be poor.

I was being practical. I convinced myself of that every day.

But now, sitting in the detective's office without the weight of those earrings and only my pink diamond winking up at me under the fluorescent lights, I realize I'm a different person. I'm not that girl who accepted this stupid pink ring. I came here on my own and solved Iris' murder for her, at the risk of losing my husband forever. He might take everything from me if this trial doesn't go through, but I know for the first time that I can handle it.

"Nella Rose," Holliday says as I stare down at our hands grasped together on the table,

"you're going to be okay."

I'm still silent and dumbfounded.

"You said he left last night, yes?" Marshall gets out a sheet of paper and a pen. "Can you tell us what kind of car he was driving and the plates?"

CHAPTER 35

June 1, 2020

Charlotte, NC

NELLA ROSE

Everyone loves a *rags to riches* story, but how often do you hear of a *riches to rags* tale that ends happily?

As I watch the movers carry my box spring mattress into my new bedroom, I look around and take in what's to be my new home for a while.

It's really not that bad. "Rags" might be dramatic, I try to tell myself, but going from my grand home in Plantation Meadows to this little rented house in Charlotte is killing me a little. There are no wood floors, no marble countertops, no farm sink, no view of the marsh.

Before Patrick was arrested, he made sure to tie up all his money so I wouldn't get a dime more than was legally required for the girls. That, combined with the small salary I was making from my blog was just enough for us to start a new life far away from Charleston. Wwell, four hours away. I also had a storage room full of antiques and wedding presents, ready to sell if needed.

Hiring a nanny on our new budget is out of the question, so both of the girls are home with me all day until Corinne starts second grade in the fall. Last year I would have been paralyzed with stress and fear if I had to keep them both by myself all day, but something woke up inside me when I realized I might be all they'll ever have.

I look down to see Eleanor tugging at my cream joggers and swiftly lift her up and bounce her on my hip. Her sweet little giggle fills the small room, and my heart aches just a tiny bit less.

"Right over there, please. Between the windows." I point out where I want the bed for the movers, then retreat to the hallway to be sure Corinne isn't getting into anything she shouldn't be.

I find her in the hallway, drawing on our gold gilded floor mirror with a dry-erase marker. She's enraptured by her artwork and doesn't even look up as I set Eleanor down and hand her a marker to join in. I never would have allowed this type of thing before—this is a very expensive mirror—but I've been working on easing up on them for little things. This marker will wipe right off.

I turn my attention straight ahead and look myself over for a moment. My highlights are growing out, and I've chopped my hair to a more manageable long bob. The stabbing pain from having my extensions ripped out still haunts me even months later. When I think about that night, which I do every day without fail, I can still feel Patrick's hands at the back of my head, the long sections of expensive hair fighting against the woven clasps connected to my scalp. The phantom sensation is too real for me, and I find myself reaching a hand to the back of my head daily to be sure it isn't real. I don't think I'll ever be able to get extensions again.

My makeup is also more natural. I turn my cheek and examine the hormonal dark spots under my eyes and around my forehead that appeared when I was pregnant with Corinne. They normally would have been covered with expensive foundation and concealers, but you can see them now through my light tinted moisturizer. No false lashes. No painted lips. I can almost recognize myself again after years of hiding my flaws.

I'm still blogging, though I don't think I realized how truly addicted I was..er..am to the rush it can give you, but things have changed with that too. I'm a mommy-blogger now, which I never thought I'd say, *ever,* and I post about easy lunches, fun and messy craft ideas and the best spots for family-friendly day trips in the Carolinas. Back when I was packing up our life in the big house, I remember realizing how much life was lacking in those grand halls. This whole time, the girls could have been playing, making messes, and enjoying their childhood rather than my constantly worrying about the mess and containing their play to their bedrooms and the backyard.

Or worrying about Patrick being upset about the mess. *Never again*, I think as I look around our new home. It's going to take time, but I'm going to get better. They only have me now.

I'm prepared for the change in my reputation once the trial begins. We were right about what Patrick's lawyers were going to do. They plan to make me out to be a gold-digging, lying, alcoholic, crazy wife, according to Taylor. I'm going to have to have to be prepared to go on the stand to tell my side of the story, she told me.

"Why hadn't you told anyone about the abuse before, Mrs. Miller?"

"You had enough, didn't you? You wanted to be free of Patrick's mistress once and for all."

"Is it true you were essentially broke when you first met Mr. Miller? I'll bet you thought putting him away would assure you got all of his assets."

"How many drinks a day do you consume, Mrs. Miller? Do you consume that many when your children are in the house?

Even if the truth is brought to light and we win, I still won't be seen the same way again. There will be people out there who will think I did all of this just to be rid of him and take all his money.

Sometimes bad publicity can still work to your advantage, like a girl I once knew who did a ridiculously old-fashioned sponsored gig for a home delivery meal company. I don't remember it completely, but the consensus from the internet was she was setting the feminist movement back 50 years by saying she wanted to have a hot meal ready for her working husband every day. Even though it pissed so many people off, she gained 300,000 followers in three weeks. Some people love to hate her; some are fans of old-fashioned marriage gender roles. Either way, it got her name out there.

I'm hoping all of this will help my name get out there as well. It would be some kind of silver lining to all of this. And who knows, Patrick could end up going to prison for life or maybe even getting the death sentence. Then, me and the girls would get everything.

Either way, it's all very uncertain. I have my pink diamond ring tucked away in our home safe in the back of my closet, just to be sure.

If Patrick gets off, I'll sell it and take the girls far away where he'll never be able to find us. I give my reflection a nod of certainty in the mirror and bend down to draw with the girls.

CHAPTER 36

June 27, 2020

Charleston, SC

VIRGINIA

"Virginia, dahlin, ah we ready to start on that gorrrgeous hair of yourhs?" My hairstylist, June, who apparently is from Savannah, Georgia circa 1925, summons me to a chair in front of a brightly-lit mirror in the bridal suite.

"Absolutely!" I chirp as I make my way over to the chair. It's blush velvet, my favorite, and I sit down carefully in my white lace robe.

Everything is going right on schedule. The bridesmaids have finished their hair and makeup, and they're going around the dining room, checking the name places on the tables. The planner is ushering around the vendors. My mother is chatting cheerfully with Mrs. Harold (who insists I call her Lorie) on a matching blush velvet couch on the other side of the suite. They both look lovely with their hair done up, and I can tell they're feeling that mother-of-the-bride and mother-of-the-groom excitement.

I'm so glad this day is finally here.

The hairstylist takes a thick lock of my heavy hair and clips it up on my head so she can start curling. I decided on a simple hairstyle for today, with just a few pieces pulled back on either side of my face so I can clip in my veil. It's a simple and delicate cathedral length veil with tiny crystals and pearls embroidered along the hem that match the design of my dress perfectly.

I can't wait to see Bennett, I think, daydreaming about seeing him standing at the end of the aisle. He's going to look so freaking handsome in his tux. Maybe he'll even cry. That's what every bride wants, isn't it?

I close my eyes as the stylist wraps more sections of my hair around the hot curling wand and let myself drift off in my own world of thought.

Things have changed a lot over the past few months.

One night in March, Bennett and I were flipping through the channels when we saw Patrick's face plastered on the local news channel.

Mount Pleasant Millionaire Patrick Miller arrested for murder of Iris Sutten.

Bennett nearly dropped the remote, trying to turn up the volume as we watched, mouths agape, a video of Patrick resisting the police while they arrested him on a highway in Key Largo, Florida. He was dumb enough to run.

That same shot played over and over again on the news for the next few months as his trial went on, and this is what we learned:

There is video proof of Patrick Miller having an affair with Iris Sutten the night of her murder.

His wife Nella Rose Miller was the one who turned in the security camera footage to the police.

Nella Rose Miller claimed Patrick Miller was physically abusive to her.

The footage showed Patrick Miller leaving his house the night of Iris Sutten's murder with a gun in his bag.

Patrick Miller was gone all night with no alibi and returned to his home two hours after Iris was found, then left the next month for Key Largo, FL.

Iris Sutten's phone is missing, and the Sutten residence had no security cameras.

Messages between Iris Sutten and Patrick Miller on the night of her death were found upon investigating their phone records.

It's really amazing the kind of secrets people can keep. I wonder if Nella Rose knew about Patrick and Iris all along and was just pretending it wasn't happening. When I had tried to confront her about it at Iris' remembrance, she had cut me off. I thought at the time she was just being rude, but now I think that maybe she did know and she didn't want to admit it to me.

Even after everything she and Iris had done to me, I still found myself feeling sorry for her a little as I watched their story on the news. I thought about reaching out to her, but I just couldn't bring myself to pick up the phone. Something made me think she still wouldn't care to hear from me.

Plus, something about all of this just seems a little off to me. It just makes me wonder if there was more to this story then she was letting on.

Also, since Iris' death, the horrible messages I was getting stopped.

It confirmed the fact that Iris was behind everything, and her fans who had hated me so much now didn't seem to care. When they found out Iris was cheating on her husband with her best friend's husband, she definitely lost her sparkle. No one can get behind something like that.

This all also made me realize something.

I was so angry with myself for spending so much time trying to be Iris' friend. I was obsessed with her, with trying to be like her, and why? Yes, I wanted to be successful, but why did it take me so long to see that even becoming her best friend and growing my account like Nella Rose would not have brought me real happiness? She was a bad person, and that's what I surely would have become as well.

Since she's been gone, my life has turned around, and I've been able to focus on what really matters; the people I love and being a good person.

My family, my friends, my husband-to-be. I've focused on my own group of nice girls, and we hang out because we actually like each other, not because we are getting anything out of it. And even though I'll never be as successful as the other girls on this app, I finally believe, down to my core, that it doesn't matter. I am enough.

I don't care about the followers anymore.

I don't care about the likes or the money or the status.

I can actually celebrate the success of the nice girls who do well, and I don't have to feel jealous of the ones who wrap their whole lives into something that isn't real. Like I did. Like Nella Rose and Iris did. We sure as hell weren't happy. None of us.

"Oh!" I'm snapped back to reality by the jab of a bobby pin in the back of my scalp.

“Oh my goodness, I’m so sahhry, Virginia! Let me fix that.” June starts frantically rearranging the pins. “I think I’m just about dohhn!”

I look up at myself in the mirror. *Wow, I look like a real bride*.

“Oh, Virginia!” My mom practically leaps across the room to get a closer look, followed by Mrs. Harold, er, Lorie. “You’re so beautiful, sweetie. Bennett is just going to die when he sees you.” My mom is already crying.

“Mom, you’re going to ruin your makeup! Is it time for me to put on my dress?” I look toward the door where our wedding planner makes her entrance right on cue.

“Yesss, it’s time!” Kaley has that chipper yet authoritative voice that makes you happily do what she says. She walks over to the window where my dress is hanging on a wire hanger that reads *Mrs. Howard,* and carefully takes it by its dainty straps.

Once I’m in the dress, it’s time to find Bennett for our “first touch.” It’s a bit of a silly but cute new tradition that lets us hold hands around a doorway while we pray or read letters to each other. It's a way of preparing for the wedding together without him seeing me before I walk down the aisle. I grab my letter to him, and Kaley leads me around the halls of the house.

We've chosen a beautiful venue for our wedding day. It's a big beautiful house right off the water, full of live oak trees, string lights everywhere, and a huge tented area for the reception. As we walk through the tent, I gasp as I take in the scene in front of me.

I had designed it all myself, with the help of the planner and the florist, but I never could have imagined it would turn out this well. I'm absolutely in awe.

We pass the elegantly set tables with blush linen runners and towering floral centerpieces in huge goblet-shaped vases. Tiny tea lights surround each vase that will light up the room when the sun goes down, but the showstoppers are the huge hanging floral displays dancing in the air above the tables. Thousands upon thousands of tiny pale pink roses are intricately woven with darker pink peonies and white tuberose in a winding and weaving pattern, hung by clear fishing wire, creating puffs of spectacular little cloud-like gardens in the sky.

I'm so distracted by the beautiful scene that Kaley has to keep reminding me to look ahead so I don't bump into any of the tables.

We reach a corridor with huge wooden double doors leading out into a brick courtyard with a little fountain in the middle, and Kaley instructs me to stand behind the door while she places Bennett in his spot on the other side. I fumble with the note I've written as I listen to the calming sound of the babbling water from the fountain. I'm a little nervous for him to read my raw emotions but excited to talk to him at the same time. All these years together have led us here, all the ups and downs, and we grew stronger through it all. It didn't destroy us. I'm so ready to be his wife.

"Virginia, okay, come over to the edge of the door but don't show yourself. Bennett is right on the other side." Kaley's voice sings as she emerges through the door. The skirts of my dress rustle beneath me as I get settled into place.

The photographers and videographers stand by on both sides to capture our little moment. I hear the click of the cameras and catch an encouraging smile from my videographer.

"Hey, baby." Bennett's low voice calls to me from the other side, and I take his hand that he's extended by the frame. We squeeze tight. I can feel his energy from here. I don't have to see his face to know exactly how he's looking right now. Handsome, of course, and a little nervous. He's probably sweating on this hot June day.

"B, I love you so much. Can you believe it's really our day?"

"I know. Seems like yesterday when I saw you across the room at that party. Imagine if I hadn't had the guts to come talk to you." His voice is shaking a little.

"I'm so glad you did." I squeeze his hand tighter. "Should we exchange the notes?"

"Yeah, but actually, um. Can we ask to have a moment alone without everyone else?"

"Um, yeah, of course. I'm sure they got enough already." I let go of his hand and go tell Kaley what we are doing, and she has the camera crews clear off. We don't have too much time if we want to stay on schedule, but I'm glad we get to have a moment alone.

It's just us. Our last hours before we're a married couple.

I walk back over to the door, "Here's my letter," I say as I pass the folded pages over to him and he takes them.

I wait a second before I ask, "Do you have mine?" He hasn't handed his over yet.

It's quiet on his side of the door for a few seconds, long enough to make the old self-conscious Virginia come back and wonder if he's having second thoughts. Maybe this was all too much for him. Maybe he doesn't want to put up with all my crap after all. I wouldn't blame him. Maybe he wants out.

"Yes, I have yours. But…Virginia. I…there's something I have to tell you…something you deserve to know before we go through with this." His voice is shaking badly now.

Of course the worst comes to mind immediately. My heart sinks.

"Babe, what's wrong. Please just tell me. Did you…did you cheat on me or something?"

He's quiet for another second. Long enough for me to start to sweat before he finally says something. He did, didn't he? He cheated with Iris, I just know it. Why wouldn't he? She cared nothing about her marriage, and she was so perfect, how could he ever say no to her if she came on to him? I guess he couldn't live with the guilt of marrying me without my knowing.

Suddenly my dress feels like it's three sizes too small.

"Bennett, just tell me."

CHAPTER 37

Feb 26, 2020

Mount Pleasant, SC

PATRICK

There's no going back after this, is there?

All the times I lost my temper on her weren't too serious to recover from. A slap here, a push there, a little bit of yelling. That was all just trivial little fights, something normal between husband and wife, and she always found a way to forget about it and move on. Return to our regularly scheduled programming.

But this feels worse.

I left her in her spot downstairs in the sunroom to calm down. She's not hysterical anymore, but she's not doing well. She wouldn't look at me even after I tried to make her.

Why did I let Iris come over here like that? I smack my fist into my open hand in frustration as I make my way up the stairs. I've been so careful all these months, and I just let her find us like that? I take two stairs at a time, hurrying up to our room.

I know this is bad. I can feel it.

It's different this time.

It's over. She's never going to forgive me. All because I had to be so stupid tonight.

I stand in the dark hallway. Do I have any options here? What are the possibilities? *Think!*

What if I just go to bed? Wake up in the morning and talk to Nella Rose and explain everything. Come clean. Her name isn't on anything—the house, the cars, the boat, the vacation home in Wadmalaw—she would have to think about all that before leaving, right? She's not dumb. She knows she would probably have to go back to working, live with the shame of a divorce, get back into the dating scene at age 29 with two daughters. That's her choice. Either stay (if I say we should work it out) or leave and lose everything. She'd be lying to herself if she didn't admit that she'd become accustomed to the kind of life I've given her. Aren't affairs just part of the deal? How can I be expected to find all that I need in one woman, especially when that slut, Iris, lives just a few blocks away? Men like me always get married, it's expected, but we just screw around a little on the side. It's just what we do.

And now, could I really stop seeing Iris? I never wanted anything complicated, just easy, but I couldn't say no to her.

Iris has some kind of sick hold on me. Every time I tried to stop things between us, she'd find a way to lure me back to her. She's everything that Nella Rose isn't. Spontaneous yet composed, classically beautiful yet sexy as hell. There's not a hint of self-doubt. She knows what she wants, and she goes for it. Yeah, a lot of her wealth comes from John, but she once told me what she was raking in with her blogging, and it's more than any woman I know.

$90,000 a quarter on average, meaning she turned a blogger career into a $360,000 a year job, and she was making more every year.

Nella Rose would tinker with her blog work and make enough money to cover her expensive online shopping bills and ridiculous beauty expenses, but it's nothing close to Iris. She just doesn't work as hard. She spends her morning boozing on Irish coffees in her sunroom and going to barre classes and happy hours when she could be at home with our kids. I never wanted her to have a career at all, but if she was going to do something, she could have at least tried to be better at it if it was going to distract her from her jobs at home.

As I think about the girls, I find myself in the hall outside their bedroom doors, Corrinne at the end of the hall and Eleanor closest to the staircase. I crack open E's door and hear the tiny ragged sound of her little snores as they rhythmically hum along with her bedtime lullaby sound machine. In the dim light from the door, I can see her button nose and chubby cheeks peeking out from her purple quilt. Her blonde hair is a mess of tangled blonde curls with a few pieces of her bangs sticking to her sweaty forehead. She always gets so hot when she sleeps.

I tiptoe across the room and kneel down beside her bed and remember the day she was born. Nella

Rose's mom had driven down to stay in our guest house the week of her due date so she could be there for the birth. Corinne was three at the time, and Nella Rose was worried sick, thinking about how we would handle getting her to the hospital with a toddler in tow, so she insisted her mom come help.

Eleanor was quick, much faster than her older sister. Nella Rose was only in labor for four hours before the doctors performed the C-section (Corrinne had been a complicated birth, and after one C-section the doctors usually do the same for any future children), and before I knew it, I was holding tiny 6-pound, 5-ounce Eleanor Legare Miller in my arms.

I remember looking around the hospital room—Nella Rose recovering in the bed in a deep and needed sleep, Corrinne coloring a picture of a stork on the floor at my feet in her pink dress with embroidered roses, and me holding the newest addition to our family all bundled up in a pink blanket, a gift from my mother who was in the hospital cafeteria with my mother-in-law getting breakfast. Her tiny red face would twist up every few minutes like she was about to cry, then she would look up at me, and I know that seeing her dad's face calmed her down.

This was the life I always dreamed of. A family. And while Nella Rose slept, I studied her peaceful face and wondered how I could ever lay a hand on her. The mother of my children. My wife.

I promised myself that day that we could turn things around. I could make her be the wife I needed so we could all enjoy this life together the way it was meant to be. I could come home from work to a hot meal on the table as my little girls ran up to me and hugged my knees. My wife would hand me my bourbon and we'd sit at the table and have a meal together. I'd sit in my chair in the living room and unwind from my long day as my wife got the kids into bed.

That's what a marriage is.

It's *not* coming home to the nanny taking care of our kids while my wife runs around town spending my money and not taking care of me or our family.

It's not having a wife who nags me and doesn't do my laundry when I need it. It's not having a wife who's too tired for sex when she hasn't done any work all day. Can she blame me for seeking it elsewhere?

I lean over and kiss Eleanor's sweaty head. She stirs a little and grabs for her dolphin stuffed animal and snuggles her face against its fuzz.

I quietly get up and retreat from the room, closing the door softly behind me.

The kids deserve better than Nella Rose as a mother, but what am I supposed to do? Yeah, Iris is what I would have wanted, but it's too late to think like that. She's not leaving John, she made that very clear, and if she intends to keep her marriage intact despite all of the mess she and I have created, I guess it's what I should do as well. We'll just see each other less, and I can go back to picking up girls at bars on my business trips in between.

I turn the other way down the hall toward our bedroom and close the door behind me, sitting on the edge of the bed, my side, closest to the window.

I have to think now.

What if Nella Rose doesn't leave? What if I convince her it was just a one-time thing? Maybe this thing with Iris would be what it takes to get her in check. She knows I could leave her, that basically I'm one foot out the door anyway, and she might be scared of losing everything. Maybe I should have revealed the affair a long time ago and she might have made some changes earlier.

I think about Nella Rose, sitting just downstairs. She saw me screwing her best friend in her own backyard. I know how she reacts to our fights, but this is unknown to me. She could take this any way. She could either be plunging into the sulky depression she normally has, or she could be angry.

Angry enough to do…what? I don't know.

She might leave with the kids, or worse.

I instinctively reach below the bed for my gun case and retrieve my revolver. If she snaps tonight, I'm not going to let it involve bloodshed. I've seen those crime shows. *Crazy scorned wife kills her children then herself.* No way, not tonight. She needs to calm down. It's the only weapon we have in the house besides the kitchen knives, but I couldn't hide those without her seeing.

I go to lock the revolver in my bedside table drawer when I feel my phone vibrate in my pants pocket. It's a text. I already know who from. I set the gun down on the table and fish out the phone to see how she's reacting to the craziness that happened earlier.

What happened with her? Iris' text reads. I have her name saved under a guy I work with, Andrew Johnson. Normally our texts are in code, things about work like, *The reports are past due* means meet me at the Point, and *He left for the meeting an hour ago* means Nella Rose is out of the house, and it's safe for her to come over.

Now that we've been found out, she doesn't bother with the code.

I write back, *She's freaking out. I don't know. Could be bad.*

She immediately starts texting back.

Patrick, you'd better get her under control. I can't have her fucking up my life because you weren't careful enough.

Me? You're the one who insisted on coming over tonight when you knew she was home. My fingers type furiously. I want to call her, but I don't want to start yelling and wake up the girls.

Don't make this my fault. You could have turned me away or taken me somewhere that's not a straight shot view from your window. Don't be a moron. Control the situation before it gets out of hand. Iris mocks me from my phone.

I'm fuming now. This cunt is going to make this my fault? She's the one who wore all those tight, low-cut outfits around me. Laughing at my jokes and getting me drunk. She basically trapped me!

Why don't we see how you handle it, Iris? I'm on my way over.

A typing bubble pops up a couple times only to disappear. She's typing her answer then deleting it. She doesn't know what to do.

A few minutes go by and no answer.

I'm definitely going over there. What could possibly make this worse? She cares so much about ruining her marriage with John and doesn't give a flying fuck that she just destroyed what was left of mine. I push myself off the bed, go to the closet and throw a few things into my backpack—a couple pairs of boxers, a t-shirt and basketball shorts—then I go to the bathroom. I click on the light and go to the his side of our his and hers sinks. I retrieve just a few things—my toothbrush and toothpaste and a razor.

I don't even know what I'm packing for or how long I plan to be gone or anything really. Nella Rose might lock me out tonight or call the police or something. I wouldn't put anything crazy past her at this point.

I exit the bathroom and am about to walk out the bedroom door when I remember the revolver. Its shiny metal is blinking at me under the light of my lamp. I walk over to the bed and tuck it into the mesh compartment on the side of my backpack and head out, down the stairs and toward the front door. It's pitch black downstairs and quiet. I'm guessing Nella

Rose cried herself to sleep in her spot in the sunroom.

Should I leave a note? Anything?

No point. I leave through the front door.

I decide to walk to Iris' house. It's only a few blocks, after all, and I don't want to risk waking up John with the sound of my Bentley.

It's a really quiet night. It has to be 3:00, 4:00 a.m., and I realize I haven't walked around outside at this time of night since I don't even know how long. Maybe college? After a long night at the bars?

In all the craziness, I hadn't thought about what a cold night it would be, and I cross my arms over my chest for warmth.

I go to turn down her road when I see it. The third house on the left. Their house isn't on the water like ours, but it's still massive and on a great piece of property. I wonder if Iris ever thought about what I could give her. What a power couple the two of us would be.

Even in my frustration with her I find myself fantasizing about what a life with her would be like.

She says she would never leave John, but she could be teasing me as usual.

We'll see what happens tonight.

As I get closer I see something laying in the road by her driveway. The street lamps aren't on, but that dull full moon is illuminating everything. It looks like a rolled-up rug or something, or maybe a deer that became roadkill earlier that night, but as I get closer I start to slow my pace. I see blonde hair blowing in the soft wind like the moss on a Spanish oak tree. Two long legs bend at the knee unnaturally, like the ones on the rag dolls Corinne plays with then tosses aside, meeting the thighs of the legs is a tiny skirt, the one I had pushed up and groped underneath just hours before.

I see a slender waist peeking out between a tiny tank top, leading up to bare shoulders and a neck, normally beautiful and elegant but now raised up and red with the traces of angry hand prints.

Then I see her face. Her scared green eyes, bugging out of their sockets. Her cheek is gently laying on the cement surrounded by her long blonde locks. The breeze blows a few strands into her face and covers her eyes.

My heart pounds in my chest, and I throw both hands over my mouth to resist from screaming.

No no no no no no no. What the fuck? What is happening? Who could have done this? Did Nella Rose call John to out us, and he killed her out of anger? Was this some random psycho? Or, maybe hit by a drunk driver? No. WHAT THE FUCK.

I can barely breathe. Is this what shock feels like? This kind of thing doesn't happen here. This kind of thing doesn't happen to people like her. What do I do?

For maybe the first time in my life, I feel helpless.

I can't stand it. I can't control myself. I kneel down without thinking and brush the hair from her face to see those eyes one last time. Those eyes which had filled me with such passion and lust and desire and hatred all at once. They aren't the same. Lifeless. Not mocking me or teasing me anymore. I wish I hadn't looked. I gently let her hair fall back over them.

Then I look to her side and see the glowing light of her phone dim in power-saving mode. I tap the screen with the back of my knuckle to wake it up and see the words of our conversation.

I stand up suddenly and look all around. My mind finally catches up. Someone just killed Iris, and from this conversation it looks like it was me. I don't have time to think things through. Someone could have heard something when it happened and called the police. They could see me right now. I grab her phone and take off running.

I run toward our house; I have to get out of here now.

I finally reach my car and jump in fast, start the car, then put it in reverse and slowly back out of our driveway. I can't be seen fleeing the neighborhood.

As I slowly drive down our street (*has it always been so fucking far away from the entrance?),* all I can think about is the Point. I can't be seen arriving anywhere right now. If a timeline of her death comes up, that'll look suspicious.

I decide to head for the Point. No one would see me there, and if I was questioned, my wife will say we had a fight and I left to get some air for the night. I'll come home in the morning because going missing will surely cause suspicion, and I can't leave without my money anyway. I have credit and debit cards on me, but I can't have it on record that I withdrew a bunch of cash tonight either.

Nella Rose will find out about Iris's murder and probably think that I had something to do with it, but what kind of person can return to his home the next day after murdering someone and act like nothing happened? Yes, that's my plan. I'll do that. I turned off the cameras before Iris came over, so there's no proof that I even left my house aside from the words of my scorned wife.

As I drive the small bridge over Shem Creek, I realize I need to get rid of the phone. I remove the SIM card and turn off the phone, then throw both pieces into the creek.

Shit, what about phone records? They'll see the phone is missing and check her correspondence.

It's over. I'm fucked. And I didn't even do it. Did someone set me up?

I have no plan, but I do know I can't run. I'll go home, and maybe they won't suspect me. I didn't touch her. I didn't do this.

CHAPTER 38

June 1, 2020

Mount Pleasant, SC

JOHN

"No, I didn't know." Hands in my face, I do my best to answer the swarm of questions directed at me from the police.

Were you and Patrick close friends?

Did Patrick ever tell you about his abuse toward Nella Rose?

Did you have any suspicion that Iris was having an affair?

Even though it's been a few months, my stomach drops at the sound of her name.

"We know this is hard for you, John. And you know this isn't an interrogation, we are just trying to get as much information as we can to help put Patrick away," Detective Holliday states as she writes something down in her notebook.

Yes, while the husband is always the first suspect in these things, I was hundreds of miles away with Ivory and my mother in Atlanta. We had a trip planned to take our daughter to visit her grandma and see the Georgia Aquarium, but Iris had cancelled that week, saying she had an important blogger event. Ivory had been so excited I couldn't cancel on her last minute, so I took her alone.

I was told there was plenty of evidence that my alibi was airtight and I was not a suspect, but who gives a fuck.

My wife is dead.

I try desperately not to cry again in front of all these people in my house, but it's no use. How will I ever live my normal life again?

You'd think that me finding out about the affair would make me miss her less, but it doesn't. I still don't really believe it. Even after they showed me all the footage of them, I don't know, it just seems unreal. Iris loved me, and I loved her. We had an amazing marriage. Surely I would have noticed a difference in the way she acted around me or talked to me. Nothing ever changed, she was just the same as when we were newlyweds.

Yes, maybe the sex had dwindled *a bit*, but isn't that normal in a marriage? I never thought it meant the love was going away. Ever. The love was always there. She could have had anyone in the world and she chose me, she wanted to be with me. I'm sobbing now.

"Okay, John. I'm sorry to have disturbed you again. I know it's going to be difficult, but I need you to be prepared to be a witness. I'm sure you must have noticed something in Patrick over the years that would help us out, right? Just keep thinking it over and we will be in touch." And with that, Holliday and the rest of the police crew stand and leave, closing the door behind them.

I want to stay in this spot forever, but I know that I can't. I make my way toward the stairs to check on the one thing that's getting me through all of this.

"Hey, Ivory? Where are you honey?"

"Daddy! Come look at me!" I hear Ivory chip from our bedroom and find her playing dress-up in Iris' closet.

Billowed around her tiny body is a long, purple dress with yards of fabric. I actually remember this one; it was from one of our maternity photoshoots we did before Ivory was born. It was just like Iris to wear something so out there. The straps hang on Ivory's miniature shoulders, and she lifts a pair of her mother's big sunglasses to her face.

"Don't I look pretty?" She tries to walk toward me but keeps tripping on the dress.

Iris' death must not have sunk in for Ivory yet. I've taken her to child therapists, thinking she will eventually crack, but so far, she hasn't cried much at all. She's been her normal self, chatting about school and friends and dance class. I'm worried that she might be holding in all her feelings, unlike me who has been letting them flow out constantly.

"Take my picture! Do I look like mommy?" she squeals, giving me a kissy face and a pose.

Robotically, I take my phone out of my pocket and snap a photo, like I had done so many times for Iris.

"Yes, sweetheart. Just like mommy."

CHAPTER 39

Feb 26, 2020

Charleston, SC

BENNETT

I roll over and look at my fiancé actually sleeping for once.

4:26 a.m. This is normally the time when she gets up and wanders around the house or goes to sleep on the couch. Her anxiety hits her like an alarm clock in the early hours of the morning, and no sleeping pills seem to help her, poor thing. I reach out in the dark and tuck a lock of her soft hair behind her ear. This tiny touch would have normally woken her up right away.

But not tonight.

I just couldn't deal with it anymore.

All the dramatics with her and Iris and Nella Rose were getting way out of hand. I don't know what the hell those bitches did to make all their followers attack her, but it just wasn't fair.

She had finally told me the story about Iris and Patrick tonight. It must have been the second bottle of wine combined with her wedding diet that did it. I didn't want to believe it at first, but Iris cheated on me back in the day, so why would she stop now?

Who does that? Sleeps with your best friend's husband? Especially when there are kids involved in both families.

Who does she think she is, destroying other peoples' lives like this? Just because Virginia told her that she thought she should come clean with John, she thinks she needs to destroy her career and attack her like this?

Hearing Virginia slur the whole story on our couch earlier tonight was just too much for me.

Here she was, getting pummeled by a lying, cheating, jealous bitch like Iris. Everything she had worked so hard for was slipping away. What kind of fiancé am I if I can't protect her?

I grabbed the half-empty glass of wine she was holding before it spilled, and excused myself to get us a refill. The talk of leaving Charleston and starting fresh had changed her mood a little, but I could tell she was still upset deep down. I didn't want to move, but I'd do it for her if it would definitely make things better, but who knows if moving was really even the solution?

I set both glasses down and looked back at her, nearly sleeping, when the idea came to mind. I said I was going to the bathroom really quick, and searched around for her sleeping pills.

I'm a doctor; I know how many of these I can slip her without hurting her, even if she's had a lot of Chardonnay. Just two capsules, plus one muscle relaxer I have hidden so she won't abuse it, and she'll be out for at least nine hours.

I'd carried them into the kitchen with me, ground them up, and sprinkled them into her wine glass. She was so drunk, she wouldn't notice a thing. Plus, it's not like she would ever expect me to do something like this. She had gulped the glass down in record speed and was out like a light.

I stare at her sleeping face, calm and free of any of her problems or worries, then carefully roll out of bed and pull on my hoodie and tennis shoes.

I walk over to her side of the bed and check her breathing one more time, grab her phone from the nightstand, then I'm out the door to the garage. I climb into my truck and start the ignition.

I've got one stop to make. I need to buy a burner phone. Nothing can be traced back to us in case she decides to file some kind of harassment charge against me. I've seen enough crime shows to know that a big guy like me going over to talk to a woman in the middle of the night can look pretty bad. Or, if Iris decides to go batshit, she might even tell Virginia I was there cheating on her. If something goes wrong, I need to make sure there's no proof I was there. Virginia would believe me over her. I think. In any case, airing on the side of safety is what you do with this much to lose.

My plan is, I'll call Iris from the phone (I'll get the number from Virginia's phone that I borrowed) and ask her to come outside and talk to me. If she really feels bad about cheating on me in college, and she has no love for her husband, maybe those old feelings will be enough for me to convince her to leave Virginia alone. I bet I could even flirt a little to help convince her, and she will eat it up. She lives off of praise.

I speed over the bridge and make my stop to buy the phone with cash at a 24-hour Walmart, keeping my hood on and avoiding any obvious video cameras. Then I'm back on the road toward Plantation Meadows when I realize I don't really know where I'm going. It's a small neighborhood, and I know she lives on the water and sort of remember what her house looks like from the times we visited (back when they were friends, or I guess when Iris was pretending to be her friend), but it's not clear. It's also going to be even harder to find it in the dark. It's 4:56 a.m., so it'll be light soon, but right now it's still pitch black.

I pull into the neighborhood and make a few turns toward the houses on the water and slowly drive by to check them out, one by one.

Holy shit. I can see why Virginia likes to come by here. These houses are freaking massive.

I continue down the street slowly, studying these houses one by one, when I see someone standing in a driveway leaning against an SUV. It's a woman, and her face is lit up from her phone screen. She looks like she's texting someone.

It's her. It's Iris.

I guess I didn't need the prepaid phone after all. But what the fuck is she doing out here so early in the morning?

Maybe this wasn't such a good idea.

No. No. I have to do this. It's no big deal. Nothing I say could make it any worse than it already is for Virginia. Things can only go up from here; I just have to play this right. I pull my truck over and put it in park in front of her next door neighbor's house.

Iris snaps her head in my direction, her phone light still gleaming in the darkness, and starts to walk towards my truck.

What's she doing? Does she recognize my truck?

I get out and softly close the door and meet her in the street around the front of the house.

"What on *earth* are *you* doing here?" Iris asks me in a low voice, but she looks back down at her phone and types more. She must be having a really freaking important conversation for her not to be giving me her full attention right now.

"I need to talk to you about Virginia, Iris," I say in a hushed tone. It's so quiet around us right now I feel the urge to whisper. She finally locks her phone and looks up at me. Without the light from her screen, I can barely make her out. I guess the street lights are turning off too early this time of year, but the moon is out and casts warm light on her face. Just enough to see her green eyes.

"Oh *please*, Bennett. Save me the sob story about how I'm ruining your *perfect* girl's life. Doesn't she have you to buy her meals? She doesn't need to be blogging, anyway." She's still whispering, but her voice has a harsh edge to it. "The only reason I was ever nice to her was because I needed her to cover for me. Well, actually, that's not the only reason."

She smiles a cruel smile as she says, "I wanted the four of us to hang out so that it would maybe give us a chance to be alone, but you never caught on to my hints. Wouldn't it have been fun? We used to have fun, didn't we, Bennett?"

What the fuck? She's just toying with me now, there's no way. I would have noticed her trying to come onto me.

"Yeah, right, Iris. Look, this isn't about me. This is about her." I take a small step back away from her moonlit silhouette.

"Whatever. Like I said, she doesn't belong in this world. This whole thing will help her in the long run to remember to stay where she's meant to be. She's, like, chubby. And from a hick family. Come on, this is Mount Pleasant, Bennett. You should understand that better than anyone." Her voice is colder than

I've ever heard it. "Really, I'm saving her from embarrassment down the road."

She has no remorse. She doesn't give a shit.

"She doesn't deserve this from you. Why are you even working so hard doing this to her if she's not a threat to you?" I say. I need to turn this conversation around; it's already not going how I wanted it to.

She cocks her head, and I think I can make out a smirk across her face. "Come on now, Bennett. It's not that. A threat? Please. And work? Ha! It's been easy. She needs to just slink back into the shadows where she belongs. Even marrying someone like you doesn't change anything about her. She's trash."

She shakes her head and looks down at her phone, which is lighting up with new texts. She opens it and stands there responding. I hear the clicks of the keyboard on her smartphone echo around us on this silent street.

"You think she's the one who's trash? Look at you, meeting up with a man other than your husband. That's what you're doing out here, right? Convenient that he's in the same neighborhood as you." I can't help myself; she's acting like such a bitch.

Iris holds her phone to her side and takes a step toward me.

"Yeah, Iris. I know about Patrick." I wonder if this was the right thing to do.

"She told you? Well… that was a *big* mistake." She's standing right in front of me now, her face inching closer and closer. "You thought what I was doing to her was bad before…she's in for a rude awakening now, thanks to you."

She lifts her hand up and presses it against my chest. What the fuck? My heart starts racing like crazy. I'm frozen. What's she doing?

"Is this really why you came here? Because, you know, I've always had a soft spot for you even after all these years." She reaches behind me and sets her phone on the hood of my truck. With the same hand, she grabs for her purse chain hanging on her shoulder and drops it to the ground. She's trying to be sexy, like a slow striptease. Both of her hands are on my chest now, and she's sliding them up to my shoulders and around my neck. Her face is inching closer, her eyes locked in my gaze. Her body is leaning into mine. Is she about to kiss me?

Before I even know what I'm doing, my hands reach up to her slender face and hold it. I look into her eyes. She might be beautiful to everyone else, but right now, all I see is ugly. She's ugly from the inside out.

I can feel her cheekbones and the shape of her sharp jaw. Her long hair is blowing softly in the breeze, and a few strands escape from behind her ear and flutter past her eyes. She's still waiting for me to give in, like I'm sure so many men before me have done. I run my hands down and cup her throat gently at the base of her neck. She exhales, closes her eyes. She's waiting for me to kiss her.

Then I feel my hands tighten, robotically. I grip her neck between them and squeeze as hard as I can. She's not even fighting, really. She's too caught off guard. She grabs at my hoodie and my arms, but it's too late for her. I see her frightened emerald eyes bulge out, red veins shooting through them. Her mouth is open wide like a fish. She's trying to gasp for air, but I know exactly where to press my thumbs for the most efficient asphyxiation, and quickly, she stops fighting. I hold on until I know it's over, until life has left her completely.

I gently lower her limp body to the ground. Even at dead weight, she's surprisingly light. I check her nails to be sure she didn't grab at my flesh at all. Looks like she only caught hold of my hoodie. She's laying there on the ground, her knees bent and arms awkwardly crumpled up by her sides. Her long hair is puddling out around her head and catching a little in the early morning breeze, the only part of her that's alive and moving.

I realize I need to get the fuck out of here. I frantically look all around me for any signs of movement or security cameras but don't see anything.

As I turn to get back into my truck, I see her phone light gleaming on the hood. I pull my sleeve over my hand as I grab it to avoid any fingerprints, and then I notice the text messages.

I don't have time to read them all, I've got to get out of here, but I do see her last text bubble from Patrick one minute ago as I set her phone next to her on the ground.

It reads, *Why don't we see how you handle it, Iris? I'm on my way over.*

The number isn't saved, but I can guess who she was waiting for out there in the cold.

I set the phone on the ground next to her. He'll find her, and hopefully he'll be stupid enough to touch her.

❀

I try to catch a ragged breath as I drive slowly back over the bridge toward home. I can't afford to get pulled over. No one can know I was over here this morning.

I'm zoned in on the road and trying to balance the millions of thoughts running through my mind. I keep replaying the image of Iris' swollen red eyes wide with shock as I took her life from her, but I can't think about it that way.

It was for Virginia. It was for Virginia. It was for Virginia.

She was the one taking Virginia's life away from her for no reason. Just because she could. Because it felt good to have that kind of power over someone.

Tonight, I was the one in power.

But it's not the same! I did it to save my fiancé from falling deep into this bottomless pit that Iris was digging for her. Iris didn't deserve to live after what she was doing to her, not to mention also to her husband and daughter. And Nella Roses' daughters.

She was a bad person who needed to not exist anymore, and no one was going to do anything about it. So, I *had* to. I just had to.

I finally make it home, head still swimming, and go straight to Virginia's side to be sure she's still okay. Her breathing is fine; she even stirs a little at the feeling of my fingers on her neck as I check for her pulse. She'll probably wake up in two or three hours.

I make my way to the backyard and collect some firewood from the back porch. Wilks stretches in his dog bed in the living room and follows me sleepily over to the fireplace. He sits next to me, nudging me with his nose to pet him, but sees that I'm busy with a task and waits patiently for me to finish.

It's a chilly February night. Nothing suspicious about a fire. I crinkle up newspaper, the old copies we keep just for this reason, and stuff them under the logs and light them with a match from a tiny blue box with *VB* on them. They're extra from our monogrammed batch order we bought as party favors to give out at the rehearsal dinner.

I sit on the wood floor and watch as the orange blazes leap around inside the brick box. They explode into the paper with a bright burst of beautiful light then dim down, leaving sad, shriveled up balls of embers and ash. Their lifetimes are short and seemingly meaningless specks of dust, but above them they have done their part. The logs flame and crackle into popping fire that will warm up the entire room in moments.

That was your life, Iris, I think. *Your life was bright and beautiful for a moment, and you served your purpose, but it was time for you to die.*

I'll always be thankful to her for being the reason I got on the map for Virginia. If I hadn't been with Iris, Virginia might never have even known who I was, and we may not have ever crossed paths at that party.

Iris also was most likely the reason why Virginia started her blog, even though she'd never admit it, and Iris definitely helped her grow it by sharing her on her page so much while they were friends.

Her flame was shorter than most, and while she lay in ashes, *Virginia* is going to be the light that shines on and brightens my world for the rest of my life.

I toss my hoodie into the fire and watch it as it's engulfed by the flames.

CHAPTER 40

June 27, 2020

Charleston, SC

VIRGINIA

My entire body is frozen as Bennett finishes telling about the night of Iris' murder.

Or should I say, the night that *he* murdered Iris.

I can't breathe. The bodice of my dress fights against my lungs as I try to take in air, but it never seems to be enough.

I step out from the doorway and open the door to reveal him on the other side. I have to look into his eyes. I have to see his face. Is this some kind of joke?

"Baby, I'm not supposed to see you." Bennett turns his face away and hides his eyes with his hands.

"Do you really think that matters right now?!" I say as I grab for his hands so he can look at me. Screw the ridiculous superstitions.

"Bennett…what…wh…are you telling me you," my voice hushes even softer now, "you're the one who k-killed her?" I'm staring straight into his dark eyes. They're pleading, wide, desperate. Different.

"I wasn't planning on it; you have to believe me. I was just going over there to talk to her, to tell her to leave you alone, and it…it just happened." He's squeezing my hands hard. I can feel his palms sweating and shaking. What's he afraid of? He's already safe. Patrick is going down for this, right?

Bennett is letting an innocent man take the blame for something he did.

"How can that just happen? How…did I not know you left?" I'm so confused as I try to recall that night. I drank a lot, I remember waking up hungover, and I remember crying to him about Iris and Nella Rose, but then we had such a nice night after that. Didn't we just go to bed?

His eyes haven't left mine. I blink at him through heavy eyelashes. He lets go of my hands and grabs my face.

A chill goes over my body as I feel his touch. These hands were wrapped around Iris' throat as she took her last breath on this earth.

"Virginia, the only thing that matters is that you're better. I did it *for you.* I just couldn't stand to watch her destroy you like that. She was the worst person in the world, and you're the very best person. She was pulling you down, and now you're free. Just *look* at how things have been for you and for us since she's been gone!"

I can barely admit it to myself, but that exact thought had been running through my mind since about a week after she was found dead.

"Do you really think that is a good excuse?"

"Please." He's pleading now. He's scared of losing me. I never realized just how much he loved me, or that the limits of what he would do for me exceeded anything I could have imagined. "Please, Virginia. Don't be afraid of me. I will never hurt you. You're my entire universe. You're...don't you see that you..."

I stand there waiting as he continues to hold my face in his strong hands.

"You are worth dying for. You are worth killing for," he pleads as I try to get a grip. I can't think. I can't just stand here like this.

"I-I have to think for a minute. This is crazy, Bennett! It's our wedding day!" I grab his wrists and free myself from his hands.

"Baby, we…I understand that this is…a lot. Please, please don't leave." He wants me to stay here and figure this out right now. How can I possibly do this? I can't even process everything right now.

"Why did you wait until right now to tell me, Bennett?! How did you think I was going to react? I don't even know who you are." I turn to go but he follows behind me.

"I had to wait! I was afraid you wouldn't marry me! And I realized I…couldn't trick you into marrying me like that; I had to tell you before, and I just couldn't get up the nerve to do it until now." A few tears fall down his face as he desperately reaches for my hands again.

"I have to…I just need a minute to think." I turn and leave him there in the hallway. I grab at the heavy skirt of my dress and run back through the dining room. The floral installations feel more like dark clouds over my head now instead of bright and wonderful sky gardens. I turn the corner and find the public ladies' room, not the one in the bridal suite.

I can't face anyone right now.

I plop onto a chaise lounge and press my hands against my temples. I can't cry, I can't let anyone see I'm upset. I just have to *think.*

He killed someone. He's a murderer.

How can I possibly go through with this?

What happens when someone else messes with me down the road? Will he kill them?

What if one day he decides I'm not as great as he thinks now? What if I mess up in some way? Will he want to get rid of me too?

What if they find more evidence and he becomes a suspect? He did it so easily. He said it wasn't even planned, it just *happened*. How can that just *happen*?

My breaths are quickening. Oh no, I don't have my pills with me. I can't let myself have an attack right now. I try to calm down and breathe more slowly, deeply. The blanket is inching over my body, weighing me down, reaching up around my neck. I need to calm down or I will have an attack right here and everyone will know something happened.

Think of something positive. That's what my therapist would say.

Things have been better for us lately. Better than ever I'd even venture to say. That's a positive, for sure.

Bennett.

And, well, this is the frightening part, the part I've been pushing back since he told what happened moments ago. If I'm being honest with myself, it doesn't scare me as much as it probably should. I keep waiting for that feeling I should be getting after hearing something so horrible about someone that I love. This is the moment where I should run as far away from him as possible, call the police, and never see him again. That's what I would tell someone else to do if they were in my position.

And yet, I'm still standing here, and I have to let myself understand why. He's not weak like I thought. He took matters into his own hands and solved my biggest problem in one fell swoop. After she died, Iris wasn't there to haunt me anymore.

What kind of husband doesn't protect his wife?

No, I can't think like that! Does that one thought make *me* the psychopath? I feel the tiny pang in the corner of my eyes from my false lashes as I squeeze them shut. These thoughts are releasing my panic, though, as twisted as they may be. So I give in to them.

I can feel the anxiety releasing me from its heavy grasp as I think about Bennett this way. A *strong* man, who would go so far as to take someone's life just because they were attacking me.

Who else in this world would do something like that for me? What would my life be like right now if he hadn't done what he did? I think about all those nights I spent balled up on our sofa, crying over the comparison and bullying and cruelty. Without him by my side, I don't know if I would have made it through.

Suddenly, the thought of losing him seems like an impossibility. I want him. I want to marry him. Everything will be all right as long as we are together. If they find evidence on him, I can be his alibi. I'll lie and say we were together all night and that he never left. They can't have that much evidence on him or they would have found it already. Patrick was the perfect cover. An abusive idiot having an affair. I don't see how this could ever be turned on Bennett.

I push myself up off the chaise decidedly and walk toward the large mirror by the door of the bathroom to check myself.

The redness on my chest is fading. My breath has calmed. It's going to be alright. I'm going to marry him.

I hurry out the door and back down the hall to find him. I have to tell him everything is okay. I can't have him thinking the wedding is off.

I push past staff members who are busy with the finishing touches on the décor. I hear Kaley's voice distant at my back, calling my name, but I ignore her. This will just take a second, then the day will be back on schedule.

As I turn down the corridor, I find him almost exactly as I left him. He's pacing back and forth, and as he hears my heels tap on the tile floor he takes off running toward me. We meet in the middle of the hallway.

"I thought I lost you," he breathes as he grabs me and holds me tightly against his chest. I don't even care if my makeup smudges.

After a moment, I hear Kaley behind me coming toward us. "What on earth! Y'all aren't supposed to see each other, is everything okay?" She's still far enough away. I have one last moment with him.

I release his embrace and reach my arms up to his shoulders. His six-foot five-inch frame still towers over me even in heels, so I get up on my tippy toes and pull at his neck for him to bring his face close to mine.

I smell his musky cologne, the same familiar scent he's worn since the day I met him.

Just like that night, in the midst of all the chaos, it's just us.

Just him and me.

I stand up a little straighter, smoothe out my dress, and inhale a breath of pure, cathartic oxygen. And I am ready. I whisper the words so only he can hear me.

"We'll talk about it later. For now, let's do this."

ACKNOWLEDGEMENTS

Brent, I couldn't have asked for a better partner in life. While I hope you never have to kill for me, I kind of know you would. Thank you for being my rock. Mom and Dad, your unconditional support of my crazy dreams never ceases to amaze me. Thank you for always being there. Madeline, our shared love of stories has made our bond so strong. Thanks for being my cheerleader. Lauren, the kindest and most selfless person I know, thank you for always being on my side. Julie, you brilliant woman, thank you for being my book nerd friend.

Lorna, Nicole, and The Yellowbird Press team, thank you for believing in me and working wonders by turning my dream into a reality.

To the rest of my friends, family, and blog followers, thank you for everything. You all are the reason I get to do what I do, and every uplifting word

I receive from you never falls on deaf ears. Thank you for buying my book and for supporting me.

Finally, to all the women out there who share this crazy career and somehow manage to stay genuine and kind, thank you.

CPSIA information can be obtained
at www.ICGtesting.com
Printed in the USA
LVHW051327100921
697437LV00009B/585

9 781733 944953